The Hot Gates

and other occasional pieces

by the same author

LORD OF THE FLIES
THE INHERITORS
PINCHER MARTIN
FREE FALL
THE SPIRE
THE PYRAMID
THE SCORPION GOD
DARKNESS VISIBLE
RITES OF PASSAGE
THE BRASS BUTTERFLY
A MOVING TARGET

THE HOT GATES

and other occasional pieces

by

WILLIAM GOLDING

A Harvest/HBJ Book
Harcourt Brace Jovanovich, Publishers
San Diego   New York   London

Preface

The following pieces are collected from those I have written during the last ten years. They are all occasional in the strict sense of the word; so that now they are to acquire some sort of permanence I have edited them slightly, removing what seems no longer applicable, and here and there removing a remark I thought plain crass.

When I brought them together I found some contaminating awareness in my mind had so adjusted them to the requirements of their varying audiences that they fell into groups which might have been the work of different writers. I cannot conceal this faint dishonesty unless I rewrite the lot, and must let it go. Where my transatlantic editors altered my spelling to conform with American custom I have let it remain so. Our system and theirs are illogical though reasonable. Why choose between them?

I ought to say a little about the piece called *Fable*. In 1962 I was asked to give some lectures at UCLA in California. The second of these dealt with aspects of my novel *Lord of the Flies*, since it had become a campus requirement. I elaborated this lecture and took it round a variety of American universities where it answered some of the standard questions which students were asking me. I print it here, in the hope that it may continue to do so.

I have to acknowledge with thanks permission to reprint articles from *The Spectator, Holiday, The Times Literary Supplement* and *The Listener*.

Contents

PREFACE   *page* 7

PEOPLE AND PLACES

THE HOT GATES   13
CROSSES   21
COPERNICUS   31
THE ENGLISH CHANNEL   41
SHAKESPEARE'S BIRTHPLACE   51
DIGGING FOR PICTURES   61
EGYPT FROM MY INSIDE   71

BOOKS

FABLE   85
IN MY ARK   102
ISLANDS   106
ASTRONAUT BY GASLIGHT   111
HEADMASTERS   116
TOLSTOY'S MOUNTAIN   121
ON THE CREST OF THE WAVE   126

WESTWARD LOOK

A TOUCH OF INSOMNIA   135
THE GLASS DOOR   140
BODY AND SOUL   145
GRADUS AD PARNASSUM   152

CAUGHT IN A BUSH

BILLY THE KID   159
THE LADDER AND THE TREE   166

PEOPLE AND PLACES

The Hot Gates

I had lunch in Lamia, a provincial town of Thessaly which lies on the route south to Athens. Most people go through Lamia without stopping, but I was following the route of the Persian invasion, that spectacular combined operation of almost twenty-five hundred years ago.

I had come down past Olympus and through the Vale of Tempe, with a classical atlas in my hand that made no mention of Lamia; so when I came unexpectedly on the town at midday, I rejoiced and thought of food. As Greek food goes, I was lucky. The time was early April, and outside every house people were grouped round an open fire. They had the Easter lamb spitted and were turning the repulsive, naked thing over the coals, hour after hour. So I ordered Easter lamb in the certainty of knowing what I would get; and it was so.

I drank *ouzo* as an apéritif, dribbling it into a tumbler of water. It tasted like licorice and looked like milk. They say you can't drink Greek water without getting typhus, but I did. There's no other way of drinking *ouzo*, and if you don't drink *ouzo* as an apéritif in a Greek provincial town, you go without.

Lamia central square was hot and dusty. The tables of the one restaurant spilled out on the pavement in the shade of some small trees. I managed to stop the waiter bringing me the wine of the country. This is *retsina*, which should be drunk once and avoided thereafter. It stinks of resin and tastes like paint remover. You must insist on an island wine, Rodos, say, or Demestica, which I got that day and liked.

It was in these parts, in 480 B.C., that the Persian army had been held up for a few days on its way to Athens. South of Lamia, the river Spercheios has cut a valley athwart the invasion route, and the road must crawl round the corner on the other side of the valley between the cliffs and the sea. Sitting beneath a

13

tree, and drinking my Demestica, I thought about Athens and Persia, and the hot springs that bubble out of the cliff where the road is narrowest, so that the Greeks call it the Hot Gates. I thought of myself too — dreaming for twenty years of coming here, poring over ancient maps; and now faced with the duty and the necessity of trying to understand.

I had seen the valley of the Spercheios when I entered Lamia, had glimpsed the vast wall of rock five thousand feet high on the other side of the valley, which lay between me and Athens. Athens was shining Athens, the Athens of history, shining in the mind. Yet when the Persian Xerxes, King of Kings, drove his army at her, she did not shine. At that time she was little but a thorn in his side, a small city which had insisted on running her own affairs — and had an odd knack of encouraging cities which ought to bow to the King of Kings to do the same.

Athens needed thirty years, and then she would shine as no city had shone before or has shone since. For all her faults she would take humanity with her a long, long step — but on that day she was nothing but a pain in the neck of the King of Kings, who had the greatest army in the world poised at her last gate.

I had *café turque* in a minute cup — one third black liquid and two thirds sludge, a delightful combination — and Greek 'Cognac'. If you have begun with *ouzo*, do not finish with Greek 'Cognac'. Even when separated by Demestica, they strike on each other like a match on the matchbox and produce a flame that does not readily die out.

I had my 'Cognac', and being English (mad dogs and Englishmen), marched out into the midday sun while the rest of Greece went sensibly to sleep. I sat down under an olive tree on the north side of the valley, where Xerxes may have stood to consider the small remaining problem before him. Mine was different. I had to re-create his problem. The Spercheios has brought so much mud down the valley that fields have pushed miles out into the sea. Where there was once a narrow pass, there is now room for road and rail, and fields that lap round the corner.

I went back for my car and drove down into the little valley and across the plain. A new motor road lies across it and sweeps round the corner where the old Hot Gates had lain between the cliffs and the sea. The road was unsurfaced, and in the rearview mirror I saw the great white cloud of dust that hung in the air behind me until it settled on the crops.

The Hot Gates were deserted. I came to an avenue and then to a group of mean-looking buildings huddled among trees. I drove in, but of course there was no one about. It was a spa, I supposed, and as far as I was concerned, on that burning afternoon, anyone who wanted a hot bath — with native sulphur — was welcome to it. I sat in the car and considered that history has left not a trace of scar on this landscape.

At the time of the Persian invasion, when the sea came close to these cliffs, the narrow track had held seven thousand men — Spartans, Thebans, Locrians, Thespians, Phocians — who watched one another as much as they watched the enemy. Greece to the south was in a turmoil as the Persians marched toward it. What to do? Whom to trust? What to believe? The track that summer was thick with dusty messengers bearing appeals for help, or accusations, or denials, or prayers to the gods. In any event, with Xerxes only a few miles away, there was a mixed force to hold the track — groups sent by the cities of Greece, and small groups at that. No city dared strip itself of troops.

Was there no memorial left? I drove out of the avenue and found one man awake at last. He was a goatherd carrying a thumbstick and a whistle. His goats were a tumultuous jumble of horns, of black and brown fur with ruffs and edgings of white, and staring, yellow, libidinous eyes. You see these herds in Greece as you may see flocks of sheep on a country road in England. Each goat has its bell, and the tinny concert, half-heard from the side of a mountain, is one of the evocative sounds of Greece. I asked him about the Hot Gates, and he pointed forward along the road. Then he turned aside with his goats and they began to file off and scatter up the side of the cliffs.

I drove on to the Hot Gates proper, where once there had been room for no more than one wagon at a time. Sure enough, there was a memorial, level with the place where that mixed force had once stood in the pass, a nineteenth-century monument, grandiose and expensive. When the battle was fought, the place where the monument stands was out in the sea.

Nature has not done her best here for the story of that battle.

The Vale of Tempe would have been a better place, and there are a hundred haunted spots in Greece where the setting would be more striking and the drama more obvious. Quiet, crop-fledged fields lie between the cliffs and the sea, with the scar of the motor road on them. The slopes and cliffs, though sprinkled with shrubs and flowers, aromatic in the hot sun, are arid with out-croppings of rock. There is dust everywhere. Little gullies leading back into the cliffs are marked with low stone walls that look ancient but are recent structures made by farmers and goatherds. If you go to the Hot Gates, take some historical knowledge and your imagination with you.

Just at the mouth of one of these gullies, I came across a mound. It was not very imposing to look at. The Greeks have planted it with laurels; but laurels planted recently in Greece never seem to be doing very well. There are some by the Springs of Daphne, some on the field of Marathon, some at Delphi — and they all look sheepish and a bit scruffy. But it was here, by this very mound, that the mixed force led by Leonidas and his three hundred Spartans came to hold the pass.

Standing by the dusty mound on that April afternoon, in the deserted landscape, where the only sound was an occasional clatter from the laurel leaves in a hot gust of wind, I wondered what Leonidas made of it all. He was, like all the Spartans, a dedicated soldier. But what did he think? As he looked north, where Lamia now lies on the hills across the valley, he must have heard the sound of quarrelling at his back. That is the one certain thing — the mixed force was quarrelling.

You can imagine the sullen afternoon lengthening, the ribaldry, the sudden shouts, perhaps even the clash of arms, the mutter of men who had to do as they were told but knew better than their leaders, the cynical laughter of men who had no faith in anything because Greece behind the wall — Athens, Sparta, Thebes and the rest — was at war not only with Persia but with itself. Then there had come a flash and glitter from the flank of the mountain across the valley.

Mark that Leonidas did not know how Athens needed thirty years to blossom. For him, Sparta, that dull, cruel city, shone brighter than Athens. But as the Persian army seeped down from a dozen pathways into the valley, and the mixed force fell silent at his back, it must have been some inarticulate and bitter passion for freedom as he knew it that kept him there, sullen and fiercely determined as he gazed across the plain.

No man had ever seen anything like this army before. It was patently unstoppable. It came along the neck of the hills on the banks of the Asopus, from the heights of the mountain and along the coastal track from Alope and Phalara. Lengthening rivers of men — Persians in fish-scale armor, turbaned Cissians, bronze-clad Assyrians, trousered Scythians, Indian bowmen, Caspians, Sarangians in bright cloth and high-heeled boots — came down and spread in a flood that filled the plain. Soon there was nothing to see but rising clouds of white dust, pierced and speckled with the flicker of steel. If each of the seven thousand Greeks should kill his ten men, there would be more than enough to press forward — and this was only the vanguard.

At their back, stretching for league after league by Mounts Pelion and Ossa, back through the narrow gorge of the Peneus to the wide plain beneath Olympus, marched the main body of the Persian war machine: Arabs in robes and Negroes in leopard skins; leather-clad Libyans, Thracians with headdresses of fox-pelt, Pisidians with their oxhide shields, Cabalians and Milyans, Moschians, Tibareni, Tacrones and Mossynoeci; Marians, Colchians with their wooden helmets, Alarodians, Saspires and Medes; and horses and oxen and mules. There were eighty thousand mounted bowmen and lancers, and chariots in a swarm no one could count.

When that assembly of nations heaved itself off the earth and marched, the ground shuddered like the head of a drum. When that assembly came to a swift Greek river and halted for miles along the bank to drink, the waters shrank to a few pools of mud. This was the army that seeped and flooded into the valley all day, and halted under its own dust before the narrow entrance of the Hot Gates.

Not a man in the pass could be sure that the rest of Greece really meant to fight. And if those panicky cities on the other side of the wall *did* combine, what could they do against such an army? And who could be sure that these lousy Thebans (or Thespians or Locrians, according to your own nationality) really meant to fight? Only the three hundred Spartans were calm, and even cheerful. They were soldiers, and nothing but soldiers, and this was what they were for.

17

Xerxes pitched his tent and set up his throne. He sent forward a scout. The Spartans saw the horseman coming but ignored him. They were bathing in the sulphur springs and combing their hair. The horseman came thumping along the plain by the shore. He turned toward them and reined back his horse just out of bowshot. He balanced there on his rearing horse and peered sideways at the pass under his lifted hand. Then he wheeled away in dust and spurts of sand. The men in the pass saw him go to a kind of glittering mound, dismount and make his report.

Xerxes waited four days — and nothing happened. The men in the pass would not recognize the obvious. On the fifth day he sent forward a troop; and the result was a pushover for the Greeks. Every time the Persians thrust them back, the Greeks simply plugged the pass more completely. He sent forward his own bodyguard, the Company of Immortals, his best troops. They were defeated. For two days the Persians attacked, and the Greeks held them.

It is said that Xerxes leaped from his throne three times in terror for his whole army. Modern historians have found this incredible, but I cannot see why. Communications between the wings of his army were primitive. At any moment, rumor could have sent those savage levies scrambling away into the mountains. If the soldiers immediately engaging the Greeks had run away, panic would have spread like a heath fire.

I strolled away from the cliff to where the modern but colossal statue of Leonidas stands on its narrow plinth beside the road. He wears a helmet and sword belt, carries a shield, and threatens the mountains with a spear that quivers slightly in the brassy wind. I thought of the messages he sent during those two days. He needed reinforcements — as many as Greece could find. But that summer the roads were thick with messengers.

And then, of course, the inevitable traitor appeared from the wings.

I moved back and peered up at the cliffs. The traitor had led a Persian force over those cliffs at night, so that with day they would appear in the rear of the seven thousand in the pass. For years I had promised myself that I would follow that track. But I should have come twenty years earlier, with knapsack, no money,

18

and plenty of breath. Yet twenty years ago I was fighting, too, and in as bitter a war. If I could climb cliffs less easily now, it was possible that I could understand war better.

I set myself to climb. The cliffs had a brutal grandeur. They were unexpectedly planless and looked little like the smooth contours I had pored over on the map. The rocks here are igneous and do not fracture along predictable lines. I clambered up a slope between thorn bushes that bore glossy leaves. Their scent was pungent and strange. I found myself in a jumble of rocks cemented with thin soil, and I glimpsed over my head the dark hollow whence they had fallen. Goat bells clittered thinly to my right. There were coarse bushes and grass, and delicate flowers bowed down to the rock with bees. There were midges, there were butterflies, white, yellow, brown, and sudden wafts of spice that took the back of the nostrils in a sneezy grip.

I put out my hand to steady myself on a rock, and snatched it back again, for a lizard lay there in the only patch of sunlight. I edged away, kicked loose a stone, disturbed another with my shoulder so that a rivulet of dust went smoking down under the bushes. The blinding sea, the snow mountains of Euboea were at my back, and the cliffs leaned out over me. I began to grope and slither down again. In a tangle of thick grass, flowers, dust and pungency, I heard another sound that paralysed me, a sound as of a rope being pulled through the little jungle under the flowers. I saw a lithe body slip over a rock where there was no grass, a body patterned in green and black and brown, limbless and fluid.

I smiled wryly to myself. So much for the map, pored over in the lamplight of an English winter. I was not very high up, but I was high enough. I stayed there, clinging to a rock until the fierce hardness of its surface close to my eye had become familiar.

Suddenly, the years and the reading fused with the thing. I was clinging to Greece herself. Obscurely, and in part, I understood what it had meant to Leonidas when he looked up at these cliffs in the dawn light and saw that their fledging of pines was not thick enough to hide the glitter of arms.

It was then — and by the double power of imagination and the touch of rock, I was certain of it — that the brooding and desperate thinking of Leonidas crystallized into one clear idea. The last pass was sold. If the rest of Greece beyond the wall did not unite and make its stand, the game was up. Leonidas knew now that he could make one last plea for that stand — a desperate plea, but one which those dull, dedicated Spartans were eminently fitted to give. I clambered and sweated down the cliffside to the place where he made it. He sent away most of his army but moved the Spartans out into the open, where they could die properly and in due form. The Persians came at them like waves of the sea. The Spartans retreated to make their last stand on a little mound.

To most of the Persian army, this must have meant nothing. There had been, after all, nothing but a small column of dust hanging under the cliffs in one corner of the plain. If you were a Persian, you could not know that this example would lead, next year, to the defeat and destruction of your whole army at the battle of Plataea, where the cities of Greece fought side by side. Neither you nor Leonidas nor anyone else could foresee that here thirty years' time was won for shining Athens and all Greece and all humanity.

The column of dust diminished. The King of Kings gave an order. The huge army shrugged itself upright and began the march forward into the Hot Gates, where the last of the Spartans were still fighting with nails and feet and teeth.

I came to myself in a great stillness, to find I was standing by the little mound. This is the mound of Leonidas, with its dust and rank grass, its flowers and lizards, its stones, scruffy laurels and hot gusts of wind. I knew now that something real happened here. It is not just that the human spirit reacts directly and beyond all argument to a story of sacrifice and courage, as a wine glass must vibrate to the sound of the violin. It is also because, way back and at the hundredth remove, that company stood in the right line of history. A little of Leonidas lies in the fact that I can go where I like and write what I like. He contributed to set us free.

Climbing to the top of that mound by the uneven, winding path, I came on the epitaph, newly cut in stone. It is an ancient epitaph though the stone is new. It is famous for its reticence and simplicity — has been translated a hundred times but can only be paraphrased :

'Stranger, tell the Spartans that we behaved as they would wish us to, and are buried here.'

Crosses

———————

Once upon a time — three or four thousand years ago, to be imprecise — there lived two kings who disliked each other. This has not been uncommon among kings even though their letters have always begun, 'Royal Brother.' But in this case there must have been something more. Though they lived a hundred miles apart, which in those days was next to infinity, they could not get along. In the end, one declared war; and when the other asked the reason, the reply he got was: 'The snorting of the hippopotamus in your ornamental pool keeps me awake at night.'

I have always felt that in those days long before the time of telecommunications, this betokened a truly royal sensitivity. Royalty has always been sensitive beyond the experience of ordinary folk. There was Queen Victoria, who was not amused. There was James I of England and VI of Scotland, who couldn't bear the sight of a knife. There was that girl too. She was very beautiful, and no matter how many mattresses she slept on, she always woke up black and blue. They were looking for the rightful heir to the throne, you see; and when they inspected this girl's bruises, they knew they had found the right one, for they had concealed a tiny pea under the bottom mattress. She was probably the daughter of the king who was kept awake by all that snorting.

Even if we commoners are of grosser material, we can each claim our particular irritant. As usual, Shakespeare summarizes for us:

> '*Some men there are love not a gaping pig;*
> *Some that are mad if they behold a cat;*
> *And others, when the bagpipe sings i' the nose,*
> *Cannot contain their urine.*'

My first and perhaps my major irritant is the barber.

21

Until I reached the age of ten or thereabouts, my father or my mother cut my hair. This was the result of comparative poverty, and of some indifference to convention. They had to catch me before they could operate, for even then I was allergic to the clippers. But they had not the professional touch; and an unfounded rumor circulated among my school friends, that my parents inverted a basin over my head and cut off anything that stuck out. Thus the word 'basin' was flung at me with that terrible jeering laugh which only small boys can employ effectively.

Later on when my father, who was a schoolmaster, referred in my class to 'the Bull of Bashan', there was an immediate howl of laughter which puzzled and disconcerted him. It disconcerted me, too, though it did not puzzle me. I prayed, with all the directness and force I could muster, to become bald straight away, but the prayer was forty years in the answering. When next my parents got out the clippers, I begged to go to the barber's, without knowing what I was letting myself in for. Since I had avoided the clippers and the kitchen chair for as long as possible, my hair was now long, and to tell the truth, somewhat knotted.

The barber sat me on a high stool and draped a white cloth around me. Then he struggled to reduce my hair to some order. He occasioned me acute discomfort — and he broke the comb. This was before the days of plastics, and the comb was of tortoise shell. In American terms, he still had to earn a quarter and had already lost half a dollar. He used language to which my priggish ears were unaccustomed, even at school. He hurled the useless fragments of the comb into a corner of the hair-strewn parlor. After that he used me ungently in pursuit of his quarter. He shoved me about and twisted my head this way and that, until with an awful pang of terror, I remembered Sweeney Todd, the Demon Barber of Fleet Street. Would I and the high stool and the white sheet drop through the floor, to be sold next day as a row of meat pies, piping hot? I got out of there with such a terror of barbers that I begged my parents to resume the contract, but they would not.

Thenceforth, I hovered between going and not going, while my hair grew like a dirty girl's, and I acquired a whole series of nicknames.

No, the barber's parlor was not my favorite place. Even when I grew older and passed that curious English barrier, the change from short trousers to long ones, I was never comfortable with barbers. A friend of mine, if he was nearly broke, would spend what he had left luxuriating in an expensive haircutting establishment, where he would be treated like a prince until they saw the size of his tip. But I could not, and cannot, luxuriate. Attention of that sort makes me uneasy or bores me. I regard that half hour in the gimbaled chair as a sheer gap in my life. *Why* does human hair have to grow in such fatuous clusters? And the victim can do nothing. If he attempts to meditate on the eternal verities — or even the temporal ones — the barber is likely to move his head into an even more uncomfortable position, so that he is aware of nothing but the hairs creeping up his nose or down his neck.

I tried to circumvent the business of barbery by growing a beard, thus avoiding the shaving part. But even this heroic gesture has its nemesis. I found that a beard has to be cut, just like the hair on my head. Moreover, I allow my beard to grow — in an effort to put off the moment when I must meet the now obsequious barber — just as I once did with my head of hair. At last, when remarks have become personal, and my beard is fan-shaped, patriarchal and very warm, I take it to the barber, who does not know what to do with it. We argue. Is it to be rounded or pointed or square or forked? Is it to be long or short or middling? I can never remember what it was like after the last visit and neither can he. It is as much trouble as a woman's hair without giving any of the same pleasure; but I am stuck with it.

In the end I leave it to the barber, grit my teeth, shut my eyes and lean back. When I open them again, I cannot recognize myself and neither can anybody else. My beard is never cut twice running alike. The contrasts are extraordinary. At the beginning, when I shut my eyes I look like something out of the Far West — a Forty-Niner, perhaps. When I open them, I am anything from a man with a goatee to the prinked and mustachioed conductor of a hotel orchestra.

Not that the barber minds, of course. He always steps back with what Kipling called 'the triumphant smile of the artist contemplating his finished handiwork'. Only the other day he summed up his joy at being given a free hand : 'There you are, sir. You came in looking like Moses, and you go out looking like Sir Francis Drake.'

But I do not want to resemble either of these eminent gentlemen. In so far as I desire anything other than immediate escape, I want to look like myself; and I do not know what myself looks like. So I smile a craven smile, give an immense tip and creep away, and as I walk toward my car, my finger is boring and twisting to find the hairs under my collar. Why do I have to do this, I think — and come to that, why do I have to wear a collar? Why am I decent only when half strangled? For though they are a subtler irritant, clothes are another daily cross for me.

Is there anything sillier, or more calculated to drive a man slowly around the bend, than a respectable suit of clothes? If you are built after the fashion of Michelangelo's Adam, you may be able to carry the burden of a suit with some air. But supposing you are not? Suppose on the contrary your tummy sticks out in one direction and your seat in the other, so that you bear a family likeness to Dickens' Mr. Pickwick? In that case, sartorially speaking, you are a lost soul. Of course, your tailor can broaden the shoulders of your jacket by inserting in them a sort of permanent coat hanger. But then you look for all the world as though you were expecting to be hung in a closet until wanted; and you don't look very much wanted.

And even your tailor can do very little about your side view. He can't build out your chest or take a slice off your back. The most he can achieve is a certain sleekness of outline, so that from the side you look like a perpendicular sea lion. After that, he puts ash catchers around the hem of each leg and provides you with numberless pockets, together with a severe injunction against putting anything in them. Finally, with all the effrontery of the accomplished craftsman, he assures you it takes forty years to learn how to fashion this monstrosity, so that you pay three times a reasonable price for it.

Who wants to see the slightly adjusted outline of an old man whose figure is beginning to 'go' like ice cream left in the sun? Society should be more charitable. Once men have started their decline and begun to gather their parcels of fat, they should be allowed to hide themselves under what clothing they choose.

24

Does anyone really believe that decrepitude can be charmed out of sight or obliterated by a tailor's sleight of hand?

It was not always so. Once, a degree of fantasy was allowable, and it gave old men the chance to preserve a proper dignity for themselves. Male clothes were as varied then as the ones women wear now. You could hide your baldness with velvet or silk or feathers or laurels. You could wear jewels in your beard. You could have shoulders of ermine, and below them a glistening cataract which gave massiveness to your body and hid your reedy legs. You could clothe yourself in the elegance and severity of a toga, so that as you walked, your feet were moving in the folds and flounces of a full skirt. For the young, there was a brave show of leg and thigh, rather than a dun-colored drain-pipe. There was the codpiece to proclaim — and if possible exaggerate — your virility. The slimness of your waist was accentuated by a belt, where hung a rapier which was little but a variation on the codpiece. You could expose your chest if you had hair on it. You could wear your hair in long curls, and finish off with a jaunty velvet cap and feather perched over one ear.

The historian will probably object that you stank. But so did everyone else. And you could always wear perfume, an aid which has been defined as 'one stink covering another'. Young men must have thought a good deal of themselves in those days; and an old one moved among them with all the dignity of a battle-ship among destroyers. But today we all wear the same uniform, the same livery of servitude to convention. Youth has not its grace, nor age its privilege. An old man exhibits his infirmities in the same clothes that do nothing but hide the graces of his grandson. We have lost both ways.

At public functions there comes a moment when I survey the rows of collar-throttled jowls and dismiss our case as hopeless. For you must be brought up in robes or fur to wear them properly. We require the ease of habit. Technicolor epics fall down on this. Even if the principal characters have some ease in their splendid costumes, there are always some supers who give away the game. There will be at least one man whose knees have the bleached-asparagus look which tells they have only recently seen the sun. Helmets in the back rank do not settle to the head but are stuck on at a variety of angles. The third councilor from the left (a speaking part; he says, 'Aye, my

Lord!') is not easy in his sandals. Nor are the bared bodies of the slaves at all convincing. They seem not only slaves, but processed, humbled structures, like a cylinder of cooked meat that has been pushed out of a tin. Their proper wear is clearly the uniform drainpipe. There is no hope or help for it. Until man is free of this drab convention and can dress as he likes, and habitually does so dress from one end of life to the other, we shall continue to button and zip and strap ourselves into a structure not much more becoming than a concrete wall, and about as comfortable.

An objector may bring forward the various magnificences of army or navy or air force uniform; and I can only reply testily that the basis of them all is the accursed suit. He may argue that academic persons, with their hoods, gowns and caps do not suffer as much as the public in general from a lack of the bizarre. But despite everything that film, television and stage show us, it is a fact that academics seldom wear academic dress. The hood hangs in a closet from one year's end to another, cellophaned perhaps, but untouched, until its fibers drag apart under its own weight. Or if it is boxed and laid flat, then the creases become permanent and end by separating the material as by so many cuts.

The academic occasion — usually a yearly one — is unrehearsed as far as costume goes. It becomes an occasion on which the faculty, at once proud and ashamed of its fancy dress, lurches through corridors and aisles in knots and clusters, covering its embarrassment and pride with occasional in-sniggers behind the hand. The less eminent will be in front; walking very slowly so as not to disconcert their seniors; and they are always disconcerted by those same seniors, who have been told to step out and are limping along very fast. There is no movement to be seen anywhere else like it, that rambling, pausing, tottering, sideways uneasy gait that has in it something of the robot and something of the drunk. For we are unrehearsed. We have had our dignity thrust upon us. It is the cross of clothes again, and we cannot bear it with dignity.

For a cross, all this is perhaps too frivolous. Consider one that is more serious: the inability to write poetry. The outsider, the man who has never tried to force words into a pattern, can have no idea of the gigantic pride of the young man who thinks he is a poet. He would not change places with a space hero. He would not change places with anyone, unless it might be another poet. When I was an adolescent, I believed myself to belong to this select company. I remember how my companions were the mighty dead who people anthologies of poetry. I remember how I would walk, or run, rather, borne on by this belief, rapt by a phrase, a concept. I remember the awe with which I contemplated my first finished set of verses and thought it was a poem. A Creative Writing Class would not have helped me; for I had a kind of virginal timidity about confessing that I had set my shoulder to this wheel. Nor, to tell the truth, could I have endured the competition of the living. I was — and now I feel a faint, middle-aged blush at the thought of it — competing with Keats and Shelley, Wordsworth and Coleridge. They never noticed, of course; which made competition all the more peaceful. When I was twenty-one, a friend sent my verses to a publisher who in a moment of blindness offered to publish them. No young man has the courage to resist an offer like that. I went on writing verse, but as publication day drew near, I cocked my ear for the sound of thunder. I wondered how big my fan mail would be.

Of course, nothing happened at all. The little book was not even reviewed. There are too many little books of verse being published, day by day, and going straight off for pulp.

Well, I went on writing verses — indeed I still do, if the urge is unendurable — though now I take no account of them — and got together another book. But there came the day, and I can only suppose it was the day on which I grew up, when I saw my verses for the poor, thin things they were. Growing up is said to be painful. I cried in a most unmanly fashion and walked where the wind dried the tears on my cheeks. I remember in a kind of valedictory way, and as a kind of epitaph, that during that walk I fashioned verses I thought would be the last I should ever make.

> *Take back, O Earth, your loan.*
> *I have sought wisdom and found none.*
> *My eyes have seen no light; my word*
> *Is blunted like a leaden sword.*
> *The book was open, but the body's rage,*
> *One by one tore out each precious page,*
> *And I am tired and I have done.*
> *O quiet Earth, take back your own.*

27

I need hardly say, the earth refused this spectacular offer. I was left then to live with the knowledge that I was just like other men, and not of the elect. Of course, the cross dwindled as time went on, until now I can wear it on a string around my neck. Only sometimes, when I meet Mr. Ransom or Mr. Eliot or Mr. Auden, I feel it burn a little.

But again, that is too serious. What cross shall I name that is middling? People who unwrap candy in the theater, people who make a noise when they eat, people who beat time to music? Advertisements that begin with a glamorous blonde and end by trying to sell you a plant for making machine tools? People who take offense too easily, people who have had their politics left to them by their grandparents, jazz, detective stories, nationalism, hereditary titles?

Bores?

Yes, bores. Certain people affect me with the same savage frustration as a visit to the barber, people who talk at the wrong moment. There are some things on television — at least on British television — that one simply *must* see and hear; one would be an oyster if one could resist them. But on the last of those occasions, there was also a program of my own on the radio which I wanted to hear because it would not be repeated. What was I to do? Tape my program? I can never make the tape recorder work. So I had mad thoughts of attending to both at once; or even of piping my own program through the television set, in the hope that a picture would improve it.

Then X and Y appeared unexpectedly: people who would get in the way of both programs and end by attending to neither. They elected television. We sat around, and as the picture came up and I resigned myself to the loss of my own program, my visitors began to talk. They said nothing worth listening to, but they talked and commented right to the end.

'. . . getting fat and losing his hair. I wonder he has the face to play this part.'

Immediately the picture contracted to postcard size, to an inane motion of puppets, mouthing like reflections in a window. My skin had goose pimples on it.

'. . . say she's going to leave her husband. But *I* think she's going to have a baby.'

Now my skin contracted like the picture. My smile felt pasted on. I had a sudden urge to hurl my visitors into the television set, make them small, mouthing puppets, and switch them off.

'. . . of course it may not *be* his baby.'

There was one psychic refuge left and I took it. This is a public confession. In such circumstances, when I cannot withdraw my mind — and I could not — I use imagination to get even with circumstances. Carefully, and with hideous intention, I fashioned two clubs from the empty air. Presently each one hung over a guest, each knotted and massive, one studded with nails, the other with slivers of obsidian. Meanwhile I smiled my false smile, nodded and shook my head, looked from the screen up into the air where my clubs hung ready, and waited for the moment of truth.

It came when my guests turned down the sound so that they could hear each other speak more clearly. I stood up. I seized a club in either hand. I became a windmill, gathering power and speed. I brought the clubs down — crash, *crash!* Blood gushed over the carpet.

My pasted smile relaxed a little.

'Would you both care for another drink?'

Barbers, clothes and bores. The last of these are more terrifying than the others. But it is a small list; and I must remember that one can usually escape from bores, even if one cannot club them. There have been times, however, when there was no escape. I once inspected the complaints of officers aboard some very small ships. Their duty was dangerous and arduous, but they made no comment on it. They made comments on each other. There were only three officers on each ship, but they lived closer together than people do in a marriage. After all, man and wife are usually apart from nine till five or later. These men could not get away. Their unholy marriage was complete and when they had any point of friction, they were like the people in Sartre's play, *Huis Clos*, whose hell it is eternally to torture each other, not with crude physical instruments like clubs, but with the sheer pressure of their individual beings. A wardroom can be much like hell, in wartime at least; and the complaints varied from a dislike of a man's morals to sheer hatred of the noise he made when he brushed his teeth.

It has become a commonplace of this century that a random

selection of people can inflict utter cruelty on one another. With the earth growing smaller, we shall need more and more protection against our small crosses. It may be that, in a hundred years, the ambition of every sensitive man will be the tranquillity of a hermit's cell.

Copernicus

The sky is the roof of human life and has been since man first lifted himself off his knuckles. He has always had ideas about that roof, and they have become more marvelous rather than less. This should confound those who believe that Change and Hopelessness go hand in hand. Who would not agree that an expanding universe with countless fires is a more wonderful place to live in than any cosmic scheme that went before it?

Yet in our pride of knowledge, we should not dismiss the most primitive concepts as the fairy tales of man's infancy. They were attempts to explain things, and they used what knowledge was available. It is a salutary exercise to think, sometimes, how we ourselves should fare if we stood where our ancestors did.

Take the ancient Egyptians, for example. If you were an Egyptian, you knew that the level of the Nile rose when a star called Nephthys' Tear fell into the river. This was a thing, like the passage of the sun across the sky, that a man could see for himself. There were ceremonies to be performed when the star fell — that is, dropped below the southern horizon — and your mind was never clear whether the ceremonies made the river rise, or whether the star would fall if the river didn't rise, and so on. There was one thing you would never think, that the position of the star and the rise of the Nile were coincidental. It couldn't be coincidence, not if you felt the unity of things, the overriding human necessity of finding a link between separate phenomena.

You were never quite sure, of course, how long the year was. You were confused by the time the sun took to get across the sky in his boat — how else could it cross all that blue, waterlike stuff? — and the time the stars took to get across it. So your

31

year was never quite long enough. You got to 365 days but were beaten by the bit left over. If a man thinks the computation should be easy, he should try doing it in ancient Egyptian, with a system of numbers even clumsier than the Roman. So the calendar was wrong and stayed that way, and the ceremonies connected with the seasons drifted farther away from them, until after about a thousand years they had worked right through the calendar. As a failure in astronomical prediction, it was spectacular.

The first step toward a rational account of the sky — one depending on observation — was taken by the Greeks. We must talk about them, since an essentially Greek view of the universe dominated Western thought until the seventeenth century. Their arguments were, as one would expect, reasonable. Clearly, the sky is the abode of God; and since God is perfect, so must the sky be. What figure is more perfect than the sphere? However you turn a sphere about its center, it remains changeless in every part. Moreover, it is obvious to naked-eye observation that the heavens are spherical. If you doubt that, go out and look at them. So all the movements in the sky must be circular, or the result of some complex of circular movements. It stands to reason. As for the spheres themselves, they must be made of some changeless crystalline substance; for they look just like that.

The man who gave definition to this system was Ptolemy, the greatest astronomer of the ancient world, who lived in the second century after Christ. His system endured without much alteration for nearly fifteen hundred years. The spheres were concentric, the moon moving in one, the sun in another, planets in yet more, and the stars in the last one on the outside. The earth was a globe at the center, motionless at the heart of all this movement. It *must* be motionless; otherwise an arrow shot straight up would not return to the bowman. When all these spheres moved over each other — since God's sky must be perfect — they did not grate like cartwheels but made heavenly music. This, too, was reasonable.

Certain wild philosophers had suggested that the earth itself rotated — had suggested, indeed, that the sun might stand still and the earth move around it, but their ideas never made any headway. The weight of common-sense opinion was too heavy, where there was no possibility of proof. This is one example of the social pressures on astronomers : even when they were ahead of the rest of humanity, they could not convince men before they were ready to be convinced. We can see in this the operation of that most mysterious and elusive thing, the climate of popular opinion. For thousands of years, astronomy *had* to accord, more or less, with the experience of the uninformed common man. No philosopher who proposed a radical change was persecuted; he was simply ignored, and his ideas disappeared or remained unread in some forgotten manuscript.

So the Ptolemaic system, with its reliance on the fairly accurate but limited ideas of Aristotle, triumphed because people were prepared to accept it as a useful summation of the universe. Nevertheless there remained unsolved problems. More accurate observation showed that only the stars have the perfect circular movement. The planets, the wanderers, do not conform to it. If you look at a planet at midnight and remember where it stood among the stars, then midnight by midnight you will see how it has shifted among them, drifting westward. In time, each planet will drift right across the sky. More than this, a planet sometimes seems to slow down, stop, reverse its direction, stop again, then drift westward once more. These movements have always seemed significant to man — but how can they be called perfect? How, in other words, can the astronomer reduce these random movements to the circular movement which alone was thought worthy of God? What is more, if he cannot account for them, he cannot predict them — and bang! goes the calendar.

Yet with all these shortcomings, there was a very good reason why the system held the field for so long. By the end of the fifth century the Roman Empire was tottering, and its fall brought in a dark age that lasted for nearly a thousand years. Men had little time or inclination to think of the physical heavens. All they wanted was security, and the finite crystal spheres gave them the feeling of it. Nor could an astronomical team assemble — astronomy has usually been a matter of teamwork, for all its many great names — because Europe was splintered and travel was a dangerous adventure. So for that thousand years, the Ptolemaic system staggered on, emended, elaborated, but never seriously questioned. Indeed, with the rise of the Catholic Church, prediction was frowned on, since it was closely linked with astrology, which seemed to deny man's free will by giving him a predestined future. Astronomy remained intellectually frozen.

There were two forces that tended all the time to unfreeze it. One was the given nature of man. Faced nightly with an appallingly beautiful and inexplicable phenomenon, some men could not but wonder, examine, speculate — though no one realized that what was wanted was an imaginative break-away from the whole system. The second freeing force was what we might call a practical matter. With the fading of the Dark Ages, commerce revived; and commerce needs an accurate calendar. The law itself was at stake. How are you going to enter into an agreement with someone for a number of years if you don't know how long a year is? Machines were being invented. Voyages of discovery were acquainting men with new places and new ideas. The speculations of the ancients were being rediscovered.

The creaking calendar had become such an irritant that the Pope himself finally looked around for a competent astronomer who was as little contaminated by astrology as possible. He settled on a canon of the cathedral of Frauenburg, who was also a doctor of canon law, a doctor of medicine, business executive of the cathedral chapter, an amateur painter, and a passionately interested astronomer in his spare time. But when the canon read the Pope's appeal to him, he asked to be excused.

The canon's name was Nikolaus Koppernigk. By birth he was either Pole or German — the argument is endless. It seems likely that Nikolaus himself would be uninterested in the question. He would have thought of himself not as a Pole or German but as a Catholic. His father was a businessman in Prussian Poland, and Nikolaus was born at Thorn; but in his youth he was virtually adopted by his uncle, the Bishop of Ermeland. From that time forward his life lay between the chapter houses of cathedrals and the high tables of the universities. He never became a priest, but always and wholly he was of the Church.

He was a serious-minded young man and very much an intellectual. Yet looking at the early portraits of him, one wonders. There is a kind of sensitivity about the face that could well belong to another sort of person. Sometimes, in the early woodcuts, he holds a lily in his left hand. One has preposterous memories of Oscar Wilde walking down a London street with a lily in his hand; and there is a minor sense in which there may be some connection. If Koppernigk was not an aesthete in the nineteenth-century sense, I believe, nevertheless, that the key to an understanding of his work is that it was *aesthetic*.

However this may be, his uncle recognized his intelligence and sent him off to be educated; and henceforth his name was no longer Polish/German Koppernigk but Latin Copernicus, as befitted a man who had joined the supremely supranationalistic organization of the Catholic Church. He studied mathematics first. Then, at the age of twenty-three, he went for further study to Bologna, where he was deflected toward astronomy by the lectures of one Domenico da Novara. This was not necessarily a profound study, since a certain acquaintance with the crystal spheres (still endlessly revolving) was a part of every young man's education. He studied medicine too, and canon law. It was a time when the sum of knowledge was not too wide for one intellect and one memory. Did not Faust take all the doctorates and apply to the devil for more knowledge when he had learned all that anyone else could teach him? But Copernicus was no Faust. Two doctorates were enough, though he was to change the world far more than Faust did. Copernicus was austere, controlled and reliable. When he went back to Poland, it was to an appointment as personal physician to his uncle.

That is the visible total of what happened to Copernicus in Italy; but there is something more hinted at, and when we know what that is, we may fancy that we can find traces of it written in his face. The Renaissance had brought to Italy all the precious wisdom of the ancient world. Men were prepared to ask questions again, perhaps even to try all things and hold fast to that which is good. Copernicus met Neoplatonists in Italy, and Neopythagoreans — men ready for the adventures of philosophical speculation with no holds barred. These men knew — for they were responsible teachers — that it was a dangerous business, not necessarily for the philosopher himself but for those little ones who might be taught; that the new ideas must go no farther than the few people qualified both to understand them and to bear their implications.

In this almost secret society, there were some who held that the sun stands still and that the earth moves around it. Today, we can find no intellectual heresy which is the equivalent of that. It would have to be a possibility known only to a handful of scientists, yet so radical and devastating that, if it got known publicly, it would overthrow society altogether. This sounds like science fiction; but it was the exact position in Europe at the end of the fifteenth century. We have no clear account of what happened in Copernicus' mind in those critical years; but it seems likely that, when he left Italy for home, he believed the sun was at the center of our system.

Here we come to the crux : *why* did Copernicus believe this? He had no proof and he had not worked out a mathematical cosmology. He was well enough acquainted with Ptolemy — or with the corrupt Latin translation of the corrupt Arabic translation of the original Greek — but he had achieved no original work. Does the key lie in the lily, a sign to initiates, perhaps, that here was a member of their society? Does it lie in the sensitive, thoughtful face? For it is the face of a poet. In Pythagoras, religion, mathematics and poetry meet. Is that not what the lily means? There was a supreme and dangerous knowledge, and initiates felt toward it as a poet feels — by intuition. Copernicus had that intuition, but he was a mathematician; the rest of his life had to be devoted to proving what he already believed.

The proof lay in the planets. So important is the idea, that we must stay with it for a while. Draw three concentric circles, and let the common center of them be the sun. The inner circle is the orbit of the earth, the next one that of another planet, and the outer one the circle of the stars. Let the earth move more rapidly than the planet. Then, by drawing lines to join various positions of the earth and the planet and extending the lines until they cut the circle of the stars, you can see how the planet will appear to move among them; and sure enough, you find that the planet appears to wander with a movement similar to the one you can observe in the sky. Copernicus committed himself to equating the results of observation to this hypothesis, because the hypothesis was an aesthetic one; a scheme not known nor proved but *felt* to be true.

Somehow, in the world of the Church and scholarship, news of his purpose, and of his plausible diagrams, got around. In that closed community, he became famous long before he published anything. He would not publish for many reasons. In the first place, he was a faithful child of the Church; before he published, she would have to approve. Secondly, for all his intuition, proof was a long time coming. Thirdly, he still believed the circle to be the perfect movement; and no matter how he rearranged the solar system with the sun at the center, still the old system of circles and circles on circles did not allow exact prediction. Worst of all, perhaps, the astronomical tables he had to use were inaccurate. Year after year, then, he fumbled with a heliocentric system and all the old spheres, trying to get them to work. We have seen how he refused to reorganize the calendar. It may be that he would have none of a system which he believed to be false, and knew himself still unable to prove the reality of his own.

Nevertheless, interest in his work was growing and spreading. He compiled a series of notes and sent them in manuscript to his friends. They were not technical notes precisely, but they showed the way his mind was moving. One copy reached Pope Clement VII; and in 1536, Nicolas Schonberg, Cardinal of Capua, wrote to him, formally ordering him to complete and publish his work.

Now it is worth remembering that all this took place in Latin, the international means of communication, which was also a kind of safety net spread between layfolk and dangerous ideas. Ideas could be caged in Latin, and as long as they never got out, none but the learned would know about them. Nor can Pope Clement or Cardinal Schonberg have worked out the implications of the new ideas; but even if they had, they would have felt secure behind Latin, and in the knowledge that to the end of time, men would have to scan the heavens with the naked eye. No one at that time could have foreseen what the world would be if the plowman as well as the priest were to find his earth moving faster than a cannon ball through empty space. It is perhaps for this reason that Copernicus worked so slowly and seemed so indifferent to fame. His proof could never be more than an abstruse mathematical argument, and his fame limited to those qualified to understand it.

His limited fame attracted pupils. There was Andreas Osiander, who was to contribute a brief foreword to his master's book. There was Erasmus Reinhold, a great compiler of astronomical tables. Most important of all there was Georg Joachim Rhaeticus, a man devoted to Copernicus personally and a famous trigonometrician in his own right. These three were young, and they urged the older man forward. It is a gleam of light in that dark age, that Rhaeticus, who was an Austrian and a Protestant, worked as pupil and friend for years with Copernicus, who was a Pole and a Catholic. The young man gave the older one his love, his enthusiasm and his energy, and at last the book was ready. It is a key book in Western thought; and by the time it was completed, Copernicus was a dying man.

The book — *Concerning the Revolutions of the Celestial Bodies* — contains two elements which it is necessary to understand. One, of course, was a detailed mathematical examination of his own system and an attempt to square it with the results of observation. This was beyond the comprehension of all but a few dozen mathematicians of his time. The system did not make prediction easier; it simply happened to be nearer the truth, and if you were attuned to the aesthetic of mathematics, you might feel that. But in the other part of his book, Copernicus made a profound tactical mistake. He tried to ignore mathematics altogether and to find some ground on which uninstructed common sense might operate. In a word, he tried to meet the arguments that might be brought against him by an appeal to common sense. In so doing, he only made it easier for the average non-astronomical, non-mathematical reader to counter him at every point. For in the days of naked-eye observation, the Ptolemaic universe was the common-sense one.

Here is an example : 'It is the vault of heaven that contains all things, and why should motion not be attributed rather to the contained than the container, to the located than the locator? The latter view was certainly that of Heraclides and Ecphantus the Pythagorean, and Hicetas of Syracuse according to Cicero.'

This gave infinite scope to those who would play at quotations. In short, his attempt to appeal to common sense was an abject failure, because no man who could not feel the aesthetic of mathematics in his bones could possibly avoid the conclusion that Copernicus was a theorist with straw in his hair.

So when the book came out, in 1543, it gathered to itself a series of uninformed criticisms which are difficult to parallel because, in a way, the event was unparalleled.

Thus a political thinker of the sixteenth century, Jean Bodin, said: 'No one in his senses, or imbued with the slightest knowledge of physics, will ever think that the earth, heavy and unwieldy from its own weight and mass, staggers up and down around its own center and that of the sun; for at the slightest jar of the earth, we would see cities and fortresses, towns and mountains, thrown down.'

Now this is very sensible, granted the kind of universe Bodin, and indeed Copernicus, inhabited. All Bodin needed was a lifetime's study of mathematics.

Martin Luther, who was used to laying down the law, dealt with Copernicus summarily in terms of Holy Writ: 'This fool wishes to reverse the entire science of astronomy; but sacred Scripture tells us that Joshua commanded the sun to stand still and not the earth.'

That is a clincher. The mind reels to think of the laborious history of other discoveries and other reassessments one would have to unravel for Martin Luther before he could have been brought to doubt the evidence of Holy Writ and his own senses.

Copernicus got nowhere once he stepped outside the world of mathematical demonstration. Only six years after Copernicus died, Melanchthon summed up the average man's reaction: 'Now it is a want of honesty and decency to assert such notions publicly, and the example is pernicious. It is part of a good mind to accept the truth as revealed by God and to acquiesce in it.'

The truth was that man's universe was about to turn inside out and explode. No man could introduce such an idea and be believed. Copernicus, in his appeal to common sense — it was really an appeal to intuition — had attempted the impossible.

The history of his idea is revealing. Again it was a matter of teamwork. His system never worked exactly. Tycho Brahe who came after him was an anti-Copernican, but he knew the value of accurate observations and spent his life compiling them. Then he produced a cosmology of his own, with the earth still at the center. Kepler, his successor, returned to the ideas of Copernicus, and at last, with Brahe's accurate observations, made them work. He got rid of the last hangover from the ancient system, the idea that movement in a circle is perfect and therefore the one movement admissible in the heavens. He went from the circle to the ellipse, and in his work we find a model of the solar system which, with minor alterations has been accepted ever since.

What was Copernicus, then? In him, the ancient and the modern meet. He inherited the work of three thousand years, and he pointed the way toward Newton and Einstein. He was, as it were, a man who lived beside a great river and built the first bridge across it.

One's mind goes back to the massive Latin book. It was forced out of him; he had no desire to publish it. His work was done in the study, in a private wrestling with problems he never thought would see the light of a larger day. It was not till the seventeenth century — when the unbelievable happened, and any man could train a telescope on the heavens and see spread before him the evidence which proved Copernicus right — that his own Church forbade his theories to be taught.

One remembers the lily. Was it not after all Pythagorean? Was it not a symbol that truth is beauty, knowledge and God? For knowledge displays no dichotomy at last, but is one. The intuition of Copernicus was the intuition common to all great poets and all great scientists; the need to simplify and deepen, until what seems diverse is seen to lie in the hollow of one hand.

They brought Copernicus his book on his deathbed. He never read it, and so he never knew that his pupil, Osiander, had prefaced it with words of his own, explaining that these considerations were theories only and not meant to overthrow the real universe established by God. Not that Copernicus would have minded much; and as he drifted away, it may well have been a sentence from his own writings that stayed with him, a sentence drawing all his work together:

'In the middle of all sits the Sun, enthroned. In this most beautiful temple, could we place this luminary in any better position from which he can illuminate the whole at once? He is rightly called the Lamp, the Mind, the Ruler of the Universe. Hermes Trismegistus names him the Visible God, Sophocles' Electra calls him the All-seeing. So the Sun sits as on a royal throne ruling his children, the planets which circle round him.'

The English Channel

W e were coming down through cloud — gray, smoky stuff so thick it seemed motionless. I stood up to stretch my legs and the curtain of cloud blinked, appeared for a moment like mountains — except that they were upside down — then whisked away, so that the air opened vastly on each side. There it was. I could see England — gray, and brown, and green — finished off neatly by the beaded strip of white cliffs. The fat man sleeping behind his cigar blocked one of the five windows with his head. Sitting down again and looking the other way — to the south — I could see the French coast, the sixty-mile sweep of the bay from Le Havre to Cherbourg. And straight down there, much nearer, was a shield of shining water.

I was glad and I knew why. Even though you quarrel with a relative, you can be glad to see him, because, through the years, he has become part of your life. This dangerous water was part of mine. I was home already. I could see what the charts had told me before, though I never really believed them on the deck of a boat. The coast of France hunched toward England opposite Dover, fell away to the south and west, then punched out the Cherbourg peninsula with its rocks and cliffs like a left hook, confining the water in a vast pool. It could be thought of as a lake. And there it was — or most of it, anyway — the heart of the English Channel. Is there any stretch of water that has been so fought and traded over, so beset with the complexities of tides and sudden storms and fog? Is there any water that can be so vast and dangerous to sail in a small boat, yet seem so small and placid when you fly across it?

Suddenly I wanted to look at my relative. I felt like a small boy in a shunting yard or among circus tents. I wanted to peer, learn and identify. I got up again and shook my head at the stewardess. 'No thanks. I'm just looking.'

41

How sophisticated the other travelers were! They gave me faint smiles or ignored me. I tiptoed foolishly, leaned and peered. What a clown they must have thought me, getting so excited over a stretch of water not much wider than the mouth of a big river. I might have explained, but of course that would never have done. After all, I am English. Mustn't speak. So I said the words with a voice inside my head, silently.

'Ladies and gentlemen, forgive me. But I am flying for the first time over — over what? I am flying over my life.'

Just down there, behind that island — under your pretty nose, madam — I saw seven (or was it eleven?) thousand ships at anchor. They filled thirty miles of anchorage. From the air, I suppose, they would have seemed separate ships. But down there, you couldn't see water — just gray paint and a wooded hill or two. We sailed south across this 'lake' to where the peninsula, with Cherbourg at its tip, was now sliding out of sight. Seen from up here, we must have seemed to ooze, the thousands of us, like a stream of dark oil. So simple a business it looked on the diagram! But the diagram did not show the darkness, the milling craft, the rising wind. Back there, in that sparkling piece of sea under the tail, I left my first lieutenant on watch and turned in, to be fresh for D-Day. He lost the whole invasion — simply mislaid it and then confessed when I came up on the bridge at two o'clock in the morning that he hadn't liked to go any faster because it was so dark.

Indeed the Channel was big that night, oceanic, and covered with a swarm of red stars from planes and gliders moving south. I found that we were miles west of our position. So we turned southeast and steamed at full speed all night over jet black waves that were showered with sparks of phosphorescence and possibly loaded with mines.

I stood there all night catching up and felt history in my hands as hard and heavy as a brick. I was frightened — not immediately of the mines we might set off at any moment, nor of the batteries ashore, nor the thousands of enemy aircraft we had been promised. I was frightened, of all things, of being late and jeered at. I find him funny now, that young man with the naval profile and the greening badge on his cap.

Yes, the Channel was wide that night. From Southampton Water to Gold Beach off Normandy was a stellar distance. But the morning and the coast together were a marvel I still cannot believe I saw. All that vanishing curve there, tucked away between the Cherbourg Peninsula and the mouth of the Seine was growing a forest of black trees hundreds of feet high. The rockets on our left fired first and one of our own planes dived straight into the first salvo.

There was the fatal geometry of his curve and the trajectory of the rockets; he touched one just as it was turning to come down. There was a bright smile of flame, the flash of a grin five thousand feet up. Then the two sides of the smile drooped away, fell, slid slowly and sadly down the sky as if it wasn't such a joke after all.

That's a dull stretch of coast from seaward. It's sixty miles of beach and low cliff with undistinguished harbors where you have to go through a lock if you want to be safe from the sea. Until it was discovered that a beach was the right place to sit in summer, no one lived there except fishermen and their women and children who picked over the rocks and eked out an existence on sea food. It was the tail end, the unwanted hedge that bounded rich French farmland. Now the seashore is an asset, but the towns and villages there are new and don't blend with their environment. If you sail from Cherbourg to Le Havre, you see them shining one after the other. You can pick out rich Deauville by the white yachts lying off the shore.

This water is the heart of the Channel. It widens all the way down from Dover until the Cherbourg Peninsula gathers it like a sleeve. The French call it the Sleeve; and we, always prone to regard a bit of water as our own property, call it the English Channel. Up here, peering from side to side and down I can nearly see the Sleeve shape. The gathered part is behind us, a sixty-mile-wide entrance to the Channel. I was once three days trying to cross that stretch in my boat and barely managed to. Away to the east, not seen, implied only by the trend of the two shores, is Dover Strait, the shoulder of the shirt — the bottle-neck. From those cliffs behind Dover I had my first sight of France when I was a child.

I saw a gray-green whale lying on the horizon, full of mystery — a patch of land that stretched all the way through the Urals, through China to the Pacific. So unreal was my picture of the world that I only glanced at the whale and was much more interested in the procession of ships making their slow way east and west.

There, where the ground was firm under my feet, where the rules were known, was home — England, the real world. Why, out there on the horizon they could not speak English, they had a president and not a king, they even drove on the wrong side of the road. That smudgy coastline might have been a picture on the wall.

Emotionally and physically, the English do not cross the Channel without great preparation. They cross it more easily and in greater numbers than they did when I was a child; but there is still a hard core of reserve. When young and untraveled, the English do not believe in the continent at all. It is a sort of fairy tale. The twenty-odd miles of water are just sufficiently difficult, require just enough enterprise and effort, to make travel in our own island the easy, obvious thing. When real storms blow up in the narrows and the ferry boats cannot run we do not think of ourselves as cut off from the French (who can still go all the way to Peking or the Cape of Good Hope by land if they choose). What is isolated is not *England* — it is Europe and Asia and India and Africa. The waters of the Channel have run for too many years in our blood.

To do them justice, the ferry services are interrupted very seldom. There are always plenty of people who travel for business or health or pleasure, so a highly specialized sea trade has grown up to serve them in the narrowest part of the Sleeve — the Straits of Dover.

Think of the problem.

The ferry has to be a sea-going ship, equipped to meet everything from the sudden storms of October to the deadly, month-long gales of midwinter. It may leave Dover in sunshine and ten minutes later be deep in fog. And then the tides in the Channel are never quite predictable. One wave rushes right round the north of the British Isles and comes down the North Sea while another sweeps up the English Channel. They meet in the narrows and ought to form a line of still water — the 'Null Point' — which should join Rye on the English coast to Boulogne on the French. But winds hold these tides back or speed them up. So the 'Null Point' flickers unpredictably. Where the tides meet, they nag and quarrel; and any wind stronger than a breeze stirs this welter into a patternless movement which is ideal for *mal de mer*.

On top of this, the twenty miles of the narrows is perhaps the world's worst water-borne traffic-jam. Every two minutes, day and night, a cargo ship passes between the cliffs of Dover and Cape Gris-Nez. Approach the narrows from any direction and you find yourself in a procession of ships. They come up the French coast from Le Havre, up the center of the Channel from the Atlantic, up the English coast from Southampton, down the North Sea from Hull and Newcastle, across it from the Baltic. Vessels from Holland and Germany pick their way past the shallows off the Scheldt and come round past Cape Gris-Nez. All these processions of traffic merge until, in the narrows, they become a crowd. Stir into this crowd the fishing boats, pleasure boats and naval craft and you can understand why disaster always threatens in the narrows. It happens every now and then, when the visibility is bad. A boat simply disappears. One was a boatload of Sea Scouts, an experienced crew with an experienced officer in charge. Last year a large ketch vanished — no one knows how, though you may guess. Somewhere in the hooting and whining gloom a high, steel bow cracked open and cut down a wooden box, unseeing, unknowing, and passed on.

It is owing to human technique and virtuosity that — touch wood — the ferries avoid disaster. They cross the streams of traffic at right angles sometimes in fog so thick that a captain cannot see the bow of his own ship, feeling their way with the delicate assurance of a blind man reading braille. Radar helps them now, but radar can be a danger too; junior officers sometimes misinterpret what shows on the radar screen. In any case, captains prefer to use their own eyes after all.

Rules For the Prevention of Collision at Sea are complex and cater mostly for the relative movement of only two vessels. But in the narrows there are always more than two. Each captain is constantly solving complex problems in co-ordinate geometry with data partly guessed at, and always facing the possibility of a sudden emergency arising out of simple human error. In fog, the need for skill is multiplied many times. Yet for three hundred and sixty-five days in the year this service, this bridge of technique and artistry, is maintained with only the rarest breaks for bad weather. You can go to sleep in a train in Victoria

Station, London, and your carriage will be loaded quietly aboard at Dover and fastened down with steel bolts as thick as your wrist. You will wake up in France, having been carried, sleeping, across the most dangerous straits in the civilized world, in the hands of one man.

How wise we were, I thought, looking out of the round window and trying to decide how far Dover was over the horizon — how wise we were not to invade Hitler's Reich by way of the narrows! He was no sailor, that man, or he would have known we should never have made it. Far better to try further west where the wide waters look more dangerous to the ignorant eye, but are rhythmical and more predictable and calmer. On the chart, what looks the shortest distance would have been the longest way home.

But then, we people who use the Channel know that we do so on sufferance; we have always understood that there are natural hazards hereabouts which are beyond man's control. If we had sailed out for the narrows, my first lieutenant could have put us slap on the Goodwin Sands. Only last summer I sailed past them gingerly in my old boat and they looked quiet enough. But they are only a mile or two off course for Calais and throughout history they have taken a constant toll of lives and ships. Even last summer, with the air full of sputniks, I saw some of the broken wrecks and knew they were recent because no ship that goes aground there stays visible for long.

The shoals are ten miles wide, center of a slow circling movement of water which the main tide keeps in motion as one great wheel turns another. The Goodwins do not merely wreck ships; they chew them up and then swallow them. The moving stones act like a system of files, mincers, teeth. The Goodwins give back nothing. Yes, we were right to invade where we did.

And yet even that wider part of the Sleeve has its perils. Last winter I drove down to the coast and out along the island to the tip of Portland Bill to watch a storm in action. I stood in the lee of a rock and an old man from the huddle of buildings by the lighthouse joined me. We watched what was left of daylight drain away while the wheeling spokes of the light burst out over the sea and swung warningly across the Race.

All the water in the Sleeve has to come past this narrower part between Cherbourg and Portland Bill, yet here there is a cliff under water. On the French side the cliff is the face of a deep gouge reaching from the Cherbourg Peninsula southwest among the Channel Islands. You can be swept down there at twelve or thirteen miles an hour to a pin-cushion of rocks where the tide rises and falls more than forty feet. But on the English side, the underwater cliff stretched away from my feet that night and the outgoing tide was running against a southwest gale. In the gathering darkness phantom lighthouses a hundred feet high rose and fell. I glimpsed for an instant a curtain of water and spray that had the shape and size of a full-rigged ship. Waves rose up and ran together and threw up a forest of smoky spindrift. This was no local spectacle, a disturbance like the commotion from a salvo of heavy shells. This stretched to the horizon. All the battleships that have ever been built would exhaust their magazines to simulate one moment of that wild abandon. We crouched in the lee of the rock, numbed. We watched the gale comb mist from the tormented water and drag it away like smoke from a burning city; and minute by minute, symbol of man's knowledge and impotence, the lighthouse sent a succession of spokes of light that swung, probed the turmoil and then flinched away as if appalled by what they saw.

Numbed and perhaps intimidated, we turned our backs on that fierce spectacle and comforted ourselves by talking. The old man had been a sailor. He had worked in the ships I remember seeing as a child, the coasting ships of small and forgotten trade routes. He had taken coal from South Wales to Newquay on the north coast of Cornwall. One of his last trips had been with china clay from Fowey to the Medway in Kent. But he was glad now to be working for Trinity House, looking after the lights on dry land. Being a sailor, at least in those days, was no sort of life. I confessed with a sort of shame that I had sailed all my life for enjoyment.

'In winter? In this sort of weather?'

No. Of course not.

A wall of difference appeared between us. He said nothing for a while, but then he began to talk and I found he was leading up to Chesil Bank. Did I know Chesil Bank?

I stalled. In fact I know Chesil Bank well. I had even helped in some rather amateurish geological investigations that had been done there. For Chesil Bank is one of the geological mysteries of the world. It is a bank of gravel, a few hundred yards wide, that stretches west from Portland, and it is slowly moving. It has come up from the bottom of the channel and sealed off more than ten miles of coast from Portland almost to Jane Austen's Lyme Regis. Between the bank and the shore are salt marshes full of wild birds, meres — shallow pools — lapping green fields and medieval villages stranded like ships. Here is Abbotsbury, with tilted houses of gray, carved stone. Here are the royal swans, beautiful, but so many as to be a pest. The bank itself is the mystery. Some juggling trick of the tides has ordained that the bank shall be a pebble-sorting mechanism which works as perfectly as an electronic sorter. At one end are boulders; and then for ten miles the pebbles are graded down in size to tiny jewel-like fragments of rounded, colored stone. If you went on the bank in fog you could tell pretty well where you were by the size of the pebbles. But to seamen this attractive exhibition is known as the Graveyard of Ships. The bank descends steeply into forty or fifty feet of water. When the prevailing wind brings in the waves they do not become lines of tumbling surf. They strike with the momentum of solid, unbroken water — with the explosive force of great guns. Sailing ships coming up the Channel had only to be a mile or two off in their estimated position to find themselves on the wrong side of Portland Bill where the bank waits. The old man talked of all this, and suddenly I realized he was telling me my favorite Channel story.

It is an old story and true, but he told it as if he had been there. He had heard it from a messmate who had heard it from a pilot who had heard it from. . . .

So the story lost nothing in the telling. It happened during one of the great storms of the nineteenth century. There was a small schooner on the run from Falmouth to Southampton. She met stiffer weather than she bargained for, stood out into the Channel for an offing and lost herself. The wind increased, beyond a gale, beyond a storm, became more or less a hurricane. At last there was nothing to do but run before it. They had only the haziest notion of where they were, thought that with luck they might be east of Portland Bill and manage to get into shelter behind the Island. A boy who climbed the foremast thought with youthful optimism that he caught a glimpse of the

Isle of Wight, but the captain knew better. They drove on before the southwest gale, reduced to a state of indifference which was disturbed only by a faint trace of hope. There are a few holes in the coast — the narrow slit of Weymouth, the lee of Portland, risky Christchurch Harbor, the mouth of Poole Harbor choked with sand. They might hit one. Things as rare have happened. But if they chanced on safety they would *be* there and *see* there at about the same time, for the storm was whipping the tops off the waves and spreading a thick curtain before them. Safety or death would be little but a glimpse and immediately after, the event. Yet when they saw something it was from some distance — the width of seven waves. They were aware first of a whiter whiteness stretching across their bows as if the sun were trying to break through in the wrong place. But then they saw that the whiteness was the fury of a wave bursting on Chesil Bank which they were about to strike fairly in the middle.

Of course, there was nothing to be done. In seconds they would crash against the face of the bank where the ship would shatter like glass. This was not shipwreck — the men would not live long enough to drown — this was summary execution. They had no time to think, only time to feel a blind and animal panic that froze them to the ropes while six waves exploded and the seventh lifted and poised the ship, ready to throw her like a stone.

The explosion never came. They were high up in the wind and spray — flying, it seemed — for one ridiculous moment. The wave was all about them, was carrying them — was putting them down — was putting them down gently, was sinking, was ebbing away.

They were afloat in the mere on the sheltered side of the bank, and ducks were swimming away from them indignantly. The stern of the schooner rested against a grassy bank. In fact, they could step ashore. A few yards away cows were standing under trees and further on there were two cottages. . . .

But already we were over England. I removed myself from memories of Portland and Chesil, gave up my defiant peering through this window and that. The trouble was, I thought, the memories were too crowded. I could not think of the Channel as a whole, or even this eastern part of it. One day I should write a book; and find, no doubt, that even one book was too little for a whole history, a whole world. Behind me, the lake, the pool of water from Cherbourg to Calais, from Portland to Dover, was swinging up to the horizon. I fumbled my way back to my seat. I remembered how the pool was fringed with the ruins of defensive works, from rusting pockets of barbed wire, back through Martello Towers and forts and castles, back to the earthworks of Bronze Age invaders. For thousands of years we have sailed these waters and wantonly added the perils of war to them until the bed of the Channel is littered thick with every kind of wreck.

And I? I have snatched my pleasure from the Channel, knowing full well that every second story about her is someone's tragedy. Perhaps that is why I never see in her the cheerful blueness that you sometimes find in open waters. At best, the Sleeve in fine weather shows an opalescence, a semi-precious beauty which has, like the gem, an overtone of menace and bad luck.

And now, in a few years, we may have a tunnel under those waters. I salute the idea. No longer will Europe and China and India be isolated in bad weather. Africa can breathe again. But as I fastened my safety belt I was still thinking of the semi-precious opal which should never be used in an engagement ring. Will those waters allow us to get away with it, to build and maintain a tunnel? Or is there still a trick or two stowed away up that ancient and capacious Sleeve?

Shakespeare's Birthplace

In the early days of the war, when Hitler was threatening to invade England, the authorities blanked out the names on signposts, to confuse German paratroopers. So about a mile from Stratford there was a large sign that read as follows:

YOU ARE APPROACHING
XXXXXXXXX
UPON
XXXX
THE
BIRTHPLACE
OF
WILLIAM SHAKESPEARE

Some cameraman with an eye for a laugh filmed this, and a year later I sat in an American cinema and listened to the giggles that spread through the audience as they got the point. I wondered then what other sign could provide such amusement. Xxxxxxxxxxx the birthplace of the Buddha? Or Xxxx the birthplace of Beethoven? We might feel a certain snobbish satisfaction in supplying the missing KAPILAVASTU or BONN; but there would be no joke to share.

I have lived nearly all my life in England, and Stratford was no more than fifty miles from my home. Yet when I was a child, Stratford was as far away as the moon — farther, indeed, for I could see the moon. To me, Stratford was the place of William Shakespeare, the burly, fancy-dress man, with the hambone frill that made such a display of his face. He was the man of the richly bound book found in every house, respected but not opened very often. He was a frequent figure in the curious half-world of children's books, the Lamb's Tales, the Children's Encyclopaedia.

His stories did not impress. They were not as brisk and telling as those of the brothers Grimm, I thought; and I see now that this was because his plots were watered down until they became nothing but straight fights between goodies and baddies, and tragedy, therefore, nothing but an example of cosmic injustice. In the badly drawn and brightly colored pictures, he sat demurely by Anne Hathaway, or held horses, or bowed from the buttocks before an idealized Elizabeth. I did not care for him much. But then I came on a song from *A Midsummer-Night's Dream* and stumbled over the words:

Hence, you long-legg'd spinners, hence!

To anyone as frightened of spiders as I was and am, this was sheer magic. I did not understand poetry but I loved incantation, whether it meant anything or not. Soon I had a store of detached lines and phrases which I treasured like seashells or fossils or stamps:

What care these roarers for the name of king?

and

What is your substance, whereof are you made?

and

Brandish your crystal tresses in the sky —

And the magician himself was born in Stratford fifty miles away. Nothing else had ever happened in Stratford before or since. Stratford was still there, frozen in time, just as illustrated. Gables leaned inward over cobbled and muddy streets. There were many horses, people in fancy-dress; it was noisy, smelly, medieval, a place of brutality and poetry.

So when I was thought roadworthy and acquired a bicycle, I rode off towards this innocently conceived picture. There was much less traffic in those days, and some of the lanes — for I took the direct rather than the main route — were little more than earthen paths between dog roses and honeysuckle. Up and down went my road, through the vale of the White Horse and over the Cotswolds, past houses and churches whose stones were weathered into the likeness of natural rock. Young, foolish, unawakened, I rode toward the revelation for all the world as though I might find the man himself leaning over his own fence, or knock on his door and be asked in.

There was sunset and then twilight, and I came to macadam and street lighting. I wheeled my bicycle between rows of houses, the Laurels, Bide-A-Wee and Mon Repos, passed a garage and petrol pumps. There were bungalows, too, each withdrawn behind a privet hedge that proclaimed private ownership without insuring privacy. Cars hooted, a train whistled and a tramp stopped me and asked for the price of a bed. I remembered how I stood, still in my innocence, and looked at a notice that said this was Stratford-upon-Avon, and how suddenly I felt shaken, dreary, and a long way from home.

Stratford has grown so much in the last fifty years that most of the approaches are encased in ribbon building. Apart from its fortune as the birthplace of Shakespeare, the town has an undistinguished history. But it is a place where people have lived for countless generations; a place where patterns of living have been trodden deep.

There were Stone Age men who fished in the Avon, and it is not impossible that we still call the river by the name they gave it. The Romans set up a villa here, and the Saxons who came after them fought on the hillside and left a cemetery behind them. But the fordable bend of the Avon drew settlers, and for hundreds of years nameless Englishmen, serfs for the most part, clustered by the bank and fought the patch of gravelly flood-plain and the encroaching forest to a stalemate.

They hung on, in a town doubtful whether it might not be a village, or even a hamlet. It did not seem to be joined to anything, for when the river flooded, the rickety skeleton of logs and planking that passed for a bridge was awash. The town looked inward, minding its own little business, a very local affair, owned and nursed by the church; and the church gave it buildings: a Guild Chapel, a Guildhall, and a great Collegiate church where the people might worship and the local worthies be buried.

Hugh Clopton put Stratford on the map. He was a native who made good, and when he became Lord Mayor of London he remembered the wooden bridge and knew there was only one way to keep in touch. He built a strong stone bridge of fourteen arches, and immediately Stratford was connected with all the highways of the kingdom. That was 450 years ago. Clopton thought the London traffic would go over it; and now all the world goes over it. The span is simple, lasting and beautiful. If Shakespeare had never been born only a few hundred yards away, some people might still go there just to look at Clopton Bridge. It was the other great thing that happened in Stratford.

Indeed, whoever you are and whatever you come for, there is plenty to see in Stratford. It is a small gridiron of streets, separated from the river by lawns and the Theater. You can walk around the old part of the town in a few minutes and learn the layout in a quarter of an hour. The show places are obvious — Shakespeare's Birthplace, Hall's Croft, where his daughter lived, and New Place, where he retired.

New Place is usually a disappointment, because nothing is left but the foundations. They are preserved in a special garden where you can find all the flowers mentioned by Shakespeare; though the ones you see have been changed by selection and breeding. He would have thought them wonderfully exotic.

One mile away is Anne Hathaway's Cottage, improbably quaint, with thatch like a racehorse's coat, and looking altogether as if it had been designed for Snow White by Walt Disney. There is also Harvard House, linked with the university; there is the Guild Chapel and the Guildhall. There is the fifteenth-century grammar school; and here we may feel firmer ground, since Shakespeare 'almost certainly' went there.

But he is so elusive and enigmatic! Very soon, among the thatch and the half-timber, the paneling and wattle, you begin to feel frustrated because these places, although connected with the name you know, illuminating nothing, put you in touch with nothing.

You move on to the church. Now at last, you think, we shall get somewhere — Holy Trinity Church, magnificent in its own right, is known around the world as the burial place of William Shakespeare. But even here the enigma pursues you. Was he ever buried here? And if he was, are his bones still here? The church had a Bone House. Grave diggers would pile there the bones they found in the graves and use the open hole for the next applicant, since burial ground was in short supply. Shakespeare would have known this. As a boy, he could well have peeped into the Bone House with a kind of horrified gusto. At any rate, he is said to be buried seven feet deep in the church, and certainly there is a curse inscribed on the slab:

> *Blest be ye man that spares thes stones*
> *And curst be he that moves my bones.*

A terse valedictory, one would think, from the world's greatest master of words; though the Lake Poets thought the lines great poetry.

But granted the author of the plays was buried under the stone slab before the High Altar — are his bones still there? Did I read somewhere in a learned journal that the grave had been excavated and nothing discovered? I have looked for the article and cannot find it. I have asked guides and they were noncommital. Then perhaps I dreamed that, in the nineteenth century, archaeologists lifted the slab and dug down *ten* feet, until their spades were in the mud of the river, and found nothing.

An effigy looks out from a niche over the grave, and most people are agreed that this fat worthy cannot be the author of *Hamlet*. I do not follow this argument. No poet I have met has looked like the popular idea of one. Those who did were would-be poets who could never achieve anything. This effigy *might* be Shakespeare, though it looks dull, didactic and bourgeois.

So the tantalizing riddle goes with us even into the church. This is the trouble with Bardolatry and Shakespeareana. For even in Stratford there is nothing you can touch and be certain that he touched it. You cannot even tread the same earth as he did. Time raises the surface of an inhabited place with refuse and rubble, so that today, when you visit an Elizabethan house, you step down into it. To walk where Shakespeare walked you would have to dig a hole in the road. The very banks of the river have shifted. 'Everything flows,' said Heraclitus, the Greek philosopher, 'and you cannot bathe twice in the same river.' So Shakespeare lived on a plane unattainable to us — almost on another planet.

It is surely this sense of bafflement that has given rise to the luxurious crop of pseudo-Shakespeares — Bacon, Essex, Marlowe. It is a sense that can send the tourist off to the Stately

Homes, all stricken by income tax and death duties, all full of real things to touch, see and admire. Or he will go to the thatched cottages of Broadway, or find another Cotswold village, full of flowers and gray stone, and sleeping in the sun like a cat.

But if you stay at Stratford for twenty-four hours, you can sample that quiet pause in the morning when the town gathers itself and prepares for what is coming. Then suddenly it seems as if the stones had given birth to people, for the streets grow crowded between one sip of coffee and the next. You find yourself speaking more loudly, since noise comes with the people, and does not stop until the last cars have drawn away from the Theater in the evening. A band plays somewhere, and the cars crawl hooting over Clopton Bridge. All at once you are aware of the faces outside the hotel window; black faces from Ghana over brilliant robes, delicate faces over rich robes from Pakistan and India, serious faces, tired faces, faces blank with too much seeing, excited faces, faces sour from cultural indigestion, faces listening, faces with mouths twisting, mouths beating the lips together in quick outlandish speech.

And if you come in the sweet of the year for the birthday, for the April celebrations, everything is even more so — more crowds, more color, more noise, more excitement. Bridge Street was two streets in Shakespeare's time, but we've knocked down the middle row and there it is, a street wide enough for a festival. When the flags of twenty countries fly over it and their ambassadors move through it in procession and the town's governing body, the corporation, marches solemnly and the band plays and the crowds swirl and babble, then, oh then, something is going on, whatever it is. You find yourself with one elbow in a Japanese rib and the other in an American, while French shoulders nudge you in the back and a Negro from West Africa splits his blackness in your face with a magnificent ivory grin.

There is a party of schoolgirls, uniformed and doing Yurrup, feverishly kept together and counted by some elegant dragon; there is the inevitable lost child crying Mamma while a red-faced copper kneels by her and tries to find out which language Mamma is likely to speak; there is the glitter of cars moving through the crowd; there are flowers and bunting and litter.

Conversation multiplies into a surge and crash as of the sea, all talking, all laughing, all singing, all band-playing, all morris dancing — yes, in England!

There are Spaniards and Russians; Australians talking an expatriated Cockney; solemn New Zealanders, nervy Rhodesians, sinewy and defensive South Africans; touchy Canadians trying to be neither British nor American and indignant that this delicate status is so seldom recognized; cheerful Norwegians and impenetrable Swedes; Americans by the busload, festooned with cameras and regarding everything — the guides, the touts, the swans, the dancers, the helicopters, the effigies and postcards, the officials, actors, reporters, scholars, tourists — with the same excited reverence.

And of course the Germans. You cannot remain long in Stratford without meeting a German, for they were the earliest and most devout of European Bardolaters. In my times they were Wanderbirds, cropped men in shorts, who carried rucksacks of impossible weight. I remember one who was poor as I was; but he had a startlingly accurate grasp of the county administration. He had also a sort of triumphant dignity, the secret complaisancy of a man who knows that one day he will rule this bit of England as a district officer.

I wonder. Has he ever come back, prosperous and middle-aged, his dreams of imperial splendors trimmed down to the enjoyment of a bank balance? Should we talk this time without the latent antagonism that smoldered under our every remark? For we were going to fight each other one day, horribly. We knew it in our bones, though our mouths did not make the admission.

I wonder what the plays meant to him then.

> Had I plantation of this isle, my lord, —
> I' the commonwealth I would by contraries
> Execute all things; for no kind of traffic
> Would I admit; no name of magistrate. . . .

Well, there were quotations enough to see him through, whatever he suffered in Tunisia, at Stalingrad or on the Rhine:

> They have tied me to a stake; I cannot fly,
> But bear-like I must fight the course.

Odd that I should remember him out of so many. There were so many Wanderbirds, solemnly pursuing whatever it was, red knees and faces, guidebooks open, doing Stratford with cheap and merciless efficiency.

The flags flap, the band plays, the morris dancers caper, the guides talk themselves into tonsillitis. The crowd is everywhere, is endless. Why do they come? They cannot all get into the Theater. You would need Wembley Stadium to contain them. What have they come for? To see the room where Shakespeare may have been born, the foundations of the house where he may have died, or the cottage where he may have done his premarital necking? He escapes this blunt approach, he defies the quick attempt to get alongside. He cannot be bought, for what he left us is not on sale in the marketplace.

You can try. You can *buy* that broad, bald head, that fattening face and pointed beard, attached to almost anything. You can stub out your cigarette on him in brass, use him as a paperweight, as the handle of a bell or a shoehorn. He decorates a bookmarker, a pincushion, looks apprehensively at you from a row of brass door-knockers. You can stir your coffee or poke your fire with him. You can use him as a brush to sweep dust into him as a shovel. He looks with an awful fixity out of one shop — as well he might, because now he is a milk jug, the top of his head prized open, while the handle sticks out of one ear and the spout out of the other. As a last affront, you can buy his face on a tea towel, and dry the dishes with him.

Now move up in the spiritual scale and see how he fares in the bookshops. He fares almost too well. Unless you are used to books about books you will wilt at the prospect: *Some Shakespearean Themes, The Shakespearean Ethic, Shakespeare's Sources, Shakespeare's Public, Shakespeare's Bawdy, Shakespeare's Birthday Book.* In the chain-store bookshop there is half a ton of Omnibus Shakespeares stacked up like a truckload of bricks. In the bookshops, the antique shops, the trinket shops, the Show Places and Museums, his picture and relevant pictures are spread out by the acre. He stands in the Elysian Fields and beckons to a dying actor. He dies himself, and bare-bosomed Comedy and Tragedy help him toward heaven — but look as if they are lifting him over a stile. His authentic Portraits eye you luminously and derisively, for they are palpably portraits of different people. And lastly, a full-sized plaster replica of his tomb effigy glares out of a dormer window with white, blind eyes that are horrible.

These are the running signs of what has been called the Shakespeare Industry. It is perhaps my fault and your fault and Stratford's fault; but certainly it is the fault of anyone who goes to Stratford only to say he has been there and to bring away the proof in his pocket. There is good in the Shakespeare Industry, a genuine reverence before the humanity of our most godlike man: but if anything is certain, it is that the heart of the approach, his precious legacy to us in this frightening world, can be nothing more than the moved experience of his poetry. Go to Stratford, as so many do, with the intention of not attending a performance in the Theater, and you offer a mortal insult to your own understanding.

Take the rest as an *apéritif*. The Shakespeare Industry becomes then a not-unwelcome setting to your enjoyment, even if the sillier manifestations of it are simply parasitic. For the industry is well organized. The bigger hotels are quaintly Elizabethan, genuinely old, and discreetly modernized. The food and the service are good; and so taut is the organization that the best way to insure getting tickets for the Theater is to book at one of the hotels, because they keep blocks reserved for their clients. Otherwise it is often impossible to get in, no matter how much you are prepared to pay. Despite the crowds that do not go, Shakespeare is still a box-office success, perhaps more so than ever before.

His plays are sometimes done better in other places, but no other place devoted to them has a standard so consistently high. A little while ago you could see *Pericles*, a collector's piece. Last season you could see *The Two Gentlemen of Verona, The Merchant of Venice, Twelfth Night, The Winter's Tale, The Taming of the Shrew*, or taste the sumptuous cynicisms of *Troilus and Cressida*. If you intend only one visit, find out what play will be on, or you might be unlucky.

From the superb to the downright bad. For it is part of the enigma that so much is bad, jostling even with the superb bits; and yet so often, the whole is an imperishable magnificence.

There is hardly a play without rant or fustian, ludicrous coincidence, a plot so broken-backed that the action sinks to earth in the middle. Time has staled the puns and obscured the allusions, turned accepted conduct into current cruelty. Today, however they are produced, his battles between six men a side are simply funny and embarrassing. We are used to Cinerama and Todd-AO, or black-and-white glimpses of the real, scarifying thing. We can no longer make this wooden ['O'] the vasty fields of France. We know a better way.

And yet, with all this against him, Shakespeare conquers you if you give him the slightest chance. There come the high moments. It was toward these moments I wheeled my bicycle so many years ago, in the ignorance of faith, and found them better than I could have dreamed. There falls a stillness on the play. The words take off. They tower into realms of feeling that no one but he has ever known how to describe.

> *Give me my robe; put on my crown, I have*
> *Immortal longings in me.*

They are moments no more to be defined than taking a Sacrament or bearing a child, or falling in love. But they are what you come to Stratford for; and once experienced they put a crown on life.

Digging for Pictures

———————⟡———————

If you examine a topographical map of England, you will see
that the Southern part of the country is dominated by a huge
starfish of high, chalk Downs, with each arm reaching out to
the sea. Once these Downs had the only roads in England —
some of the oldest roads in the world. They are very little used
now. They are simply wide tracks between hedges or wire
fences, their surfaces turfs sometimes as perfect as the lawns
of an Oxford college. A shepherd and his flock, a solitary walker
smoking a pipe and glancing at his map, a man on horseback or a
drover with his cows — this is the only traffic you will meet.
Once the valleys below the Downs were full of forests and
swamps, but the iron ax and the iron plow cleared them; and
then the Romans briskly drove their military roads from
one end of the country to the other and dictated the future
shape of English history. The old roads on the Downs were
forgotten.

Where they meet, at the center of the starfish, was a prehistoric metropolis; and the cathedral of that metropolis was
Stonehenge. The whole of this area is sown thick with the
remains of ancient peoples. To spend your life here in Wessex,
as I have done, is to live where archaeology is as natural, or at
least as usual, as gardening. Walk across a newly plowed field
and you may pick up a stone spearhead which has not been
touched by human hand for 20,000 years. As crops come up, you
may be able to detect rows of plants which grow faster than the
others — because they have more room for their roots in a
forgotten and earth-filled ditch. That ditch is part of a camp lost
3,000 years ago, which thus emerges in shadowy outline until
the rest of the crop catches up and the whole thing vanishes
again. If you take your children for a walk, they may play 'king
of the castle' on a grassy mound, without knowing that a king is

already in residence below them, his calcined bones huddled in an earthen pot, the rest of his kingdom forgotten.

Of course our professional archaeologists are as brisk as the Romans were. You can see them often enough on the Downs. They dig and survey with infinite precision. They map and dissect, docket and assess. You see them using the delicate devices of their science — surveying instruments and mysterious boxes which do strange things with the earth's magnetism. They ponder, lost in thought over a map, while the west wind tumbles a mop of scholarly hair. They crouch in square holes, hour after hour, brushing the dust away from finds with camel's-hair brushes. They publish diagrams of digs, statistical analyses of pottery fragments and photographs of sections of the earth with each stratum labeled. They are very efficient. Their published minds never run away with them. They are austerely proof against the perils of exercising an imagination which might assume too much.

We amateurs are allowed to help them sometimes — under strict supervision. But I have never had the courage to admit to a professional that, as far as I am concerned, archaeology is a game, and that I would not dig if I was unable to let my mind run riot.

For me, there is a glossy darkness under the turf, and against that background the people of the past play out their actions in technicolor. Sometimes I feel as though I have only to twitch aside the green coverlet of grass to find them there. Might I not come face to face with that most primitive of Europe's men — Neanderthal Man — who once loped along the track where I used to take my Sunday walk? This sort of thinking is, of course, the rankest amateurism. It is to think like the Welsh, who say that King Arthur still sits inside Mount Snowdon, playing chess with his knights and waiting for the last battle.

For most of us, though, history is not diagrams — however accurate — but pictures; and in a place like this, the pictures lie under the grass, where our spades reach for them into the loaded soil. Do not the old men in the pub farther up my village talk of the golden boat that lies in the mound on top of the hill? Of course that must be a legend — but a golden boat *was* found under just such a mound in Sweden.

DIGGING FOR PICTURES

Of course our archaeologists have done a splendid piece of work, accurate and sober. They have established whole periods of prehistory in outline. But we amateurs are not like them. We are antiquarians. We are akin to those nineteenth-century parsons and squires who would take the family, a wagon and a dozen bottles of port or sherry onto the Downs and make a picnic of digging. Awful was the damage they did, 150 years ago, digging, for the hell of it, into the burial mounds of kings. Yet year by year life lays down another layer of remains for tomorrow. We amateurs can even envy them their careless rapture. Our lawless hearts leap, not at a diagram, but at the luck of the villager who turns up a cache of golden ornaments with his plow — wonderful, barbaric ornaments which will go into a museum, but should gleam on some lovely throat or wrist. Gold dies in a museum despite all you can do. All the gold that Schliemann dug up at Troy looks no better than tinsel, under glass.

Yet it was a local man who started the rot — or, as I suppose I had better say, who transformed the ancient game of the antiquarian into the modern science of the archaeologist. That man lived just over the hill outside my window, at an estate called Cranborne Chase. He was General Augustus Henry Pitt-Rivers, a character who contributed his own legend to the countryside. He was, in fact, one of the English eccentrics. We have had many such and they enliven our history, though they were an expensive way of getting results. General Pitt-Rivers stocked his park with rare animals, for instance, so that a poacher after a brace of pheasant might suddenly find himself surrounded by the mysterious shapes of kangaroos. He built a bandstand and gave concerts to which his tenants were obliged to come. He got interested in the mounds and ditches on his estate, and, at one stroke, paved the way for archaeology to become a science. He made it a military operation. He employed regiments of laborers, surveyors and young scholars. He measured and recorded everything he found — whether he understood what it implied or not — so that today, almost a century later, his results can be interpreted without fear of a mistake.

How strange the mind is! Pitt-Rivers tried to discover the history of his estate and all its petty kings; yet for me, at any rate, he has obscured it. Consider. In the early days of spring, General Pitt-Rivers would set out, in a vehicle drawn by two splendid horses, through the cuckoo-haunted woods. His coachman drove, in fully livery, and two grooms sat with folded arms at the general's back. Behind them, pedaling madly through the white dust, came his squad of young scholars, whom we may now call archaeologists, and who each achieved eminence and fame as such in later life. They rode penny-farthings, bicycles so named because their front wheels were so much larger than their rear ones. They wore tweedy trousers, blazers or Norfolk jackets, and straw boaters emblazoned with the general's colors.

Pitt-Rivers was a man of terrible authority. He had the body of the earth laid open for him as a surgeon might order an intern to make the first incision. No one has ever claimed that he was a likable man, and no one has ever doubted that he had some of the madness of genius. Yet his zoo and his band, his museum perched ridiculously on top of the Downs, near Farnham, his extravagant archaeology, his savage personality — these have obscured that same shadowy past he tried to illuminate. For if I walk over his estate I do not think of Stone, Bronze or Iron Age men. I find myself listening with my inward ear to the tramp of laborers in step. I hear the busy clatter of hoofs, and half-shrink into the hedge as I imagine the general bustling by; and behind him comes that learned covey of riders on penny-farthings — their solid tires bouncing over broken flint — each with a hand up to hold on his ridiculous, emblazoned hat.

But the land is aglow with every kind of picture. When our children were small, we used to take them to some woods which hang on the side of the Downs and seem as impenetrable as those which surrounded the Sleeping Beauty. They are deserted except for the fox and wood pigeon. But if you step aside from the country lane you find that a deep ditch leads up into them — not a dug ditch, but one of these smooth grooves, three yards deep and ten yards wide, which can be made by nothing but generations of feet.

Trees lean in and form, over the groove, a green tunnel. Nobody walks there now. Yet it is as visibly an ancient main road as is the Pilgrim's Way which Chaucer followed across the green hills of Kent. Only when you have clambered along it for hundreds of yards do you see why it is there — and where it once led. The woods have grown up around and through an immense building. Its walls and roofs are down. There are blocks of masonry; there is a gable still standing; there are the stumps of pillars, outlines of rooms, corridors, halls. Beneath your feet is grass, but underneath it you feel the firmness of pavement. You stand in the plan of a hall and see that worn steps lead down from one end, and you have some sense of the myriad feet that scooped away their stone.

You wait, but nobody comes. At most you hear a distant shriek of laughter from the woodman's children, who are climbing trees far away in the forest. Meadowsweet and nettle, old-man's-beard and purple loosestrife compete with the leaning oaks to shut away the world. The noisiest thing in the whole humpy, huddled ruin is the flight of bees. The worn steps will wait a long time for feet.

'My Palace of Clarendon,' said Henry the Second, 'Clarendon, which I love best of all places in the world.'

The mind takes a sudden dive. Eight hundred years ago this place, tree-shattered and lost in the forest, was the center of our world. You could not have stood on this grassy pavement then, for the men-at-arms would have hustled you away. You might perhaps have sneaked to the door — there, where old-man's-beard has made a sunproof thicket — and watched the jugglers performing on a feast day before the high table. You could have begged for scraps over there, where a mountain ash has forced two blocks of stone from the lintel; and if you came for justice, you would have got it here, however long you had to wait your turn. For the Law was given here — the greatest gift a nation can hope to have. But to get that justice, no air has ever been torn as these few cubic feet of air were torn by mortal passion. For, on the pavement which still lies three inches below the grass, Henry the Second and Saint Thomas à Becket stood face to face. When my daughter could just about walk, she found a piece of medieval glass here, a fragment iridescent as a soap bubble, and my mind fogged with the effort of realizing that the King or the Saint might have drunk from it.

The history of Clarendon is too crowded for the mind. You come up out of your imagination to an emptiness where the wood pigeons talk to each other and the steps wait, year in, year out, for feet. That is the trouble with what you might call official ruins. The mind needs a more personal stimulus than these acres of stone. Nor can we imagine a king or a saint. It is ordinary people to whom we reach out in imagination.

For this reason I prefer the humdrum in digging. I do not expect to dig up the Magna Charta — do not need to, since it lies, at the moment, nine miles away from me in Salisbury Cathedral. I do not expect to find Arthur lying beside the sword Excalibur under Mount Badon. My pictures are more intimate and less important. I like to pick through the ashcans of the Iron Age and guess how life went on. Digging, I lay my hand on things. I discover an immediacy which disappears when the find becomes official and is displayed behind glass. Just as the gold of Troy has lost gloss, so a bone or a stone dies a few moments after you lift it from the earth. But nevertheless, for those few moments, obscurely and indefinably, you feel a connection with the past.

This is where the specialty of our Downs comes in. Round any ancient settlement are hundreds of pits which have been filled in so completely that you can find them only when you can recognize the faint depression which is sometimes left. Those clever people of two or three thousand years ago used to scoop out a bottle-shaped pit in the chalk and line it with wickerwork and clay. This made a convenient silo for grain. But after a few years the silo would be contaminated with fungus, so they would move off a few yards and dig another. Now when you consider that this went on for as much as 500 years, you can see that wherever the Downs were inhabited they must have been stippled like the skin of a trout.

But the old silos were not left empty. They became excellent rubbish pits, into which anything unwanted was dumped. Digging in them, you do not find inscriptions or careful burials; you find only the records of daily life. And, since the pits are multiplied by the thousands, you are unlikely to destroy anything which would be of value to the serious archaeologist. He may use them to work out the number of inhabitants and the duration of the settlement; but he need only excavate a pit here and there. The pits, in fact, provide the amateur archaeologist with an equivalent to the practice slopes for skiers.

First, after you have broken up and laid aside the hard earth, you will find bones of sheep or oxen, bones sometimes of deer or the tusks of a boar. They were good meals, and the marks of the knife are still on them. Time is kind to bones. It cleans them with an intimate care which cannot be duplicated even in the laboratory. Every delicate line, every ridge and pocket, lies there in your hand, so that the bones have a strange, functional beauty. And as you concentrate, leaning down, free of archaeological diagrams and statistics in your private world, it is strange if you cannot put the meat back on the bone and the whole joint, hissing and spluttering, on the dish which lies in fragments below you. For of course these pits are full of broken pottery. I do not know whether it is a failing of mine or a virtue that I am never able to see these fragments as clues in a dating series. My private world falls in fragments, like a pot, when the presiding archaeologist leans down into my pit and defines the pottery.

'Early Iron Age. I thought it would be.'

No. Crouched in my pit, I hold the fragment in my hand and enjoy it. Presently Dr. Stubbs will investigate it closely through his bifocal lenses; and then it will be presented in a plastic bag to Miss Wilson, who will record it in a ledger. But here and now, as I lift out the triangular fragment with the two sharp edges, I get a sort of warm domesticity from it. This is not very old pottery. It is very new. It was thrown in here five minutes ago. Holding the piece in my hand I can just make out voices.

Owen, bach, look what you've done! Clear it up now — go on! Not another mouthful do you eat until the pieces are in the pit and the hearth as clean as a new leaf!

Those large lumps of chalk are loom weights. They hung in a thumping, swinging row, to keep the warp straight; they must have been wonderful playthings for small children round their mother's feet — as attractive as a swallow to a cat, and providing a most mysterious place to hide in, behind them, as mother threw the shuttle and the length of unbleached cloth crept down toward the earthen floor.

67

Here is the flint scraper which she used for cleaning leather. Her mother used it before her, for the flint itself is worn away. This is the very bone needle she was using yesterday to sew leather. I know she used it to sew leather because there is that subtle shine you only get round a point that has pierced many times through oily skin. Of course that shine will dull in the museum. Indeed it dulls after only a few moments' exposure to the air, so that when I see the needle again under glass I shall wonder how I ever knew so much about it. But for the few seconds after I lift it out, I know it was used only last night. What was she sewing — Gwyneth, Olwen, Myfanwy — at the door of the hut, when the Downs were mysterious with level rays of sun? Somehow it is more important to know that than to know about kings and priests and emperors.

Next to the needle is a spindle whorl cut out of chalk. Not many months ago, I saw women using just such spindle whorls in the wilder parts of Yugoslavia. You tuck the distaff, with its head of raw wool, between your left arm and breast. The spindle whorl turns, hanging on an end of thread; and as you mind the sheep you draw down the thread and spin it between finger and thumb. All day long you do that, when you are not rubbing down corn on a saddle stone or grinding it in a rotary quern. . . . It is possible to work very hard and be very happy.

These are innocent pictures. Yet I must remember, after what happened, that if we try in history to do nothing but escape from a corrupt present these pictures will be what we want them to be, rather than the truth. I must remember in particular the time when excavation left me with something like a load of guilt.

We were doing a 'rescue dig'. The biggest airplane in the world — at that time — was coming to live on our Downs, and required a concrete runway several miles long. The runway, as it grew, pointed straight at the scene of an Iron Age settlement which had never been examined. We set to work, chased by cement-pouring machines. We dug feverishly, trying to wrench a few facts out of the earth before concrete buried them six feet deep. I was given an old silo to dig, because a quick look through their rubbish would confirm the picture we had built, from other sources, of this people's mixed farming and hunting. Pottery, too, would enable Miss Wilson to date the settlement. For others, there were the foundations of huts, with irregular postholes; work which required the professional touch.

I dug with the tongue of concrete protruding toward me. The sense of hurry itself made me stubborn. I did not think the earth-shifting machines, the smoothing machines, the cement mixers and pourers would ignore me when they came to the lip of my pit. Moreover there was an indefinable sense of pathos in bringing this family to life for an hour or two, only to leave them and their innocent existence to be swallowed up forever. I found myself lingering. I paused to re-create, to enjoy myself in yet another tenuous contact. There was, I remember, a piece of chalk which might have been the head of a doll; but if ever there had been a rag or leather body, it had vanished. There was a spindle whorl only partly finished. You could see how the disc had been bored from both sides and how the maker had given up before the hole was complete. There was a mass of ashes and mortar, and a broken saddle quern. There was pottery too, of course, and piles of bones — the usual bones which I could have predicted, after these years of digging. But history must make certain.

Down in the dark and quiet pit, once more I made contact. Here they were again, another family from the days of innocence. Howsoever wicked they may have thought themselves, I gave them absolution. They could not match our wickedness. Above the roar of the advancing machines, I heard them speak.

The lump in the middle of the pit clearly covered something big and interesting. I attacked it with enthusiasm, as if it were going to bring me face to face with them. I was surprised, therefore, when the lump proved to be bone. There were two bones that were articulated. I traced a long bone up to a pelvic girdle, to vertebrae and ribs.

It lay sprawled. It was, I believe, an old woman. One arm was twisted behind her back, and her legs were splayed. Her beautiful skull was full of earth, and the pits that decay had made in her teeth had been cleaned out by time, to a gemlike perfection. Her jaws were wide open, grinning, perhaps, with cynicism at the fact that no one had troubled to close them.

I, and the phantom family, crouched over her. Only yesterday they had come here, laboring through the heather to the rubbish pit with their slack burden and flung it in. What kind of people were we, that we could go on living only a few yards away and fill the rest of the pit year by year with kitchen waste and broken pots?

'We've got to leave. Are you finished?'

I leaped up in a kind of terror. The machines were looming over us. I scrambled out, stood between Doctor Stubbs and the pit, and babbled at him.

'Yes, yes. It's all out. There it is — bones, pot, loom weights, quern. . . . No, there's nothing more to be done!'

Only when the approaching bulldozer had thrust the pile forward and the earth had fallen back into our pit with a long, silken swish did I feel a kind of easiness. The whole dreadful family was back underground. But even beneath six feet they have taken something of me with them. Now I confess, for the first time. Perhaps it is not so good an idea to try to penetrate temporal boundaries and identify yourself with people without first knowing what sort of people they are. There is a sense in which I share the guilt buried beneath the runway, a sense in which my imagination has locked me to them. I share in what was at the least a callous act — in what at the worst may very well have been a prehistoric murder.

Egypt from My Inside

When I was seven, I wanted to write a play about Ancient Egypt — not the Egypt of the Badarian predynasts, or of Ptolemy and Julius Caesar, or of General Gordon; but the Egypt of mystery, of the pyramids and the valley of the Kings. Half way through the first page of my scrawl, I was struck by the thought that these characters ought to speak in Ancient Egyptian, a language with which I was unacquainted at the time. I abandoned my play therefore and started to learn hieroglyphics; so that I cannot now remember when those sideways-standing figures, those neat and pregnant symbols were not obscurely familiar to me. My inward connection with Egypt has been deep for more than a generation. When my mother took me to London, I nagged and bullied her to the British Museum; and if I think of London now, that museum, with the rich Egyptian collections is at the heart of it.

I do not wish to claim that my interest has been one of exact scholarship or painstaking science. The work of scholars and scientists has brought up massive information which denies the mystery. They are all children of Herodotus, the first Egyptologist. It is entertaining to meditate on Herodotus in Egypt. He was the first, for example, to point out the peculiarly dense quality of the Egyptian cranium, and he brought forward statistical evidence for it. He inspected an ancient battlefield and tried Egyptian skulls against those of their opponents as a child might strike one pebble on another. He found that in every case, the Egyptian skulls were the more durable; a fact he attributed to their habit of shaving the head and exposing it to a nearly vertical sun. Later, the guides showed him some statues of women with their hands lying on the ground before them. They told him these were women who failed to preserve the virtue of a princess, and had their hands cut off as punishment. There the

71

matter might have ended had Herodotus been a decent, credulous tourist. But he insisted on examining the statues for himself. He found that the statues were wooden, that their hands had been pegged on, and in course of time had dropped off. The legend died with a whimper. It was a meeting between two opposite psychic worlds — perhaps even a meeting between two ages. It was commonsense and experiment at odds with vivid imagination and intellectual sloth.

I salute the Herodotean method grudgingly and am wary of it. It is a lever which controls limitless power, but a power in which I am not much interested. The method has begotten that lame giant we call civilization as Frankenstein created his monster. It has forgotten that there is a difference between a puzzle and a mystery. It is pedestrian, terrible and comic. Because it both bores and frightens me, I laugh at it, and find my image of it in a half-witted countryman and the way he made a discovery. He stood there with his beer, describing his first day-trip to London. He dropped statement after statement into the ruminative silence. He told how a nice young lady spoke to him in the street. Very friendly she was. She took him to her flat, where she gave him a meal and such a strong drink that he missed his last train. Then — would you believe it? — she gave him half her bed; and such was her social perception and delicacy that she didn't wear a nightie, because he had no pyjamas. In the morning, this kind young lady gave him his breakfast, and a warm hug at the door — .

At which point in his story, he stopped suddenly, took the mug of beer from his lips and cried, with a mixture of astonishment and conviction: 'Eh! If oi'd played moi cards roightly, I could 'ave 'ad that wench!'

In dialectical terms, this is an example of the change of quantity into quality, the laborious collection of information which may eventuate in a new theory of the whole. Those to whom the method is their only tool are as dull as they are laborious. They will decide, for example, that a statistical survey of the desiccated bodies of predynastic savages in desert sand, leads them to believe they have discovered the source of the Egyptian conviction that the body would be resurrected and therefore must be embalmed. This is an interesting theory, and relevant, I suppose, to the lurching progress of human society.

It gives to desiccated flesh a kind of material dejection, as if it were the body of a dog. What it is not relevant to, is the child, looking down on dry skin and bone, and hearing for the first time a brassy yet silent voice inwardly proclaiming: *That is a dead body; and in course of time that is what you will become.*

I must admit that the Egyptians themselves were partly to blame. They did not always deal with mystery. They declined whenever possible from high art and preoccupation with first and last things into a daylight banality. The ponderous self-advertisement of their pharaohs, the greed of their tomb robbers, the cruelty of their punishments, the dullness of their apothegms, are understandable and recognizable in modern terms. How at home we feel with the foetid Victorianism of some of the trinkets that littered the tomb of Tutankhamen! We recognize as almost contemporary, the dull portraits of stupid burgers with their stupid wives. It is the sort of thing we might very well do ourselves. It is not much worse than the average advertisement or the average television programme. It means no more either. Even on a higher level than this, the level of supreme craftsmanship, the Egyptians are likely to present us with an art we can see round, accept as a notable statement of the transience of life and no more. Look at the gold face mask of Tutankhamen. It is beautiful, but there is weakness in the beauty. It is the face of a poor boy, sensitive perhaps and idealized, but vulnerable. It looks at us, and for all the marvellous trappings of royalty, we see that death is a final defeat. The gold shapes no more than the sad lyricism of Herrick:

> *Fair daffodils, we weep to see*
> *You haste away so soon.*

It was not by this I was caught as a child. Indeed, in those days the boy still lay undiscovered in his tomb. Certainly I was attracted — as who is not? — by the time-stopping quality of the place and the climate. I delighted in the copper chisel, left in a quarry five thousand years ago but still untarnished and shiny in that dry air. I found poignant immediacy in a schoolmaster's correction of a copybook text. That classic story, the prints of the last feet to leave the tomb still visible on the floor in a scattering of sand, shut time up like a concertina. Yet though I learned as much as I could of the language and the script, memorized king lists and all the enneads of the gods, these things remained peripheral. I must go back down the years, remember what it was like, and find out what I was after.

There is a museum dusk and hush. It is a winter night and visitors are few or none. I have had my nose to a showcase for two hours. I have listed and drawn every object there, every bead, vase, fragment, every amulet, every figure. I have pored over the blue faience Eye of Osiris until that impersonal stare has made me feel as still and remote as a star. The *Ded*, that tree trunk for which the method will one day find a Freudian explanation, seems to me a veritable Tree of Life. I know about symbols without knowing what I know. I understand that neither their meaning nor their effect can be described, since a symbol is that which has an indescribable effect and meaning. I have never heard of levels of meaning, but I experience them. In my notebook, the scarab, the ankh, the steps, the ladder, the *thet*, are drawn with a care that goes near to love.

It seems to me, as I lean over the case, that I might get somewhere — as if I, or someone, at least, might break through a crust, an obscuration into a kind of knowledge. That feeling makes me hold my breath — turns my fascination into a kind of desperate struggle, an attempt to achieve a one-pointedness of the will. Yet what am I after? What am I trying to discover? For it is not merely a question of symbols. As I back away, I know there is something else beyond the glass of another showcase which is vital to me — something, a language perhaps, a script of which these beads, figures, amulets, are no more than the alphabet. Man himself is present here, timelessly frozen and intimidating, an eternal question mark. Let no one say there is nothing to a mummy but bones and skin. Reason tells us one thing; but a mummy speaks to a child with a directness that reason cannot qualify. The mummy lies behind glass, and not a visitor passes without stopping to look sideways with an awed and almost furtive glance. He commands attention without movement or speech. He is a brown thing, bound in brown bandages, some of which have flaked away, to show parchment, a knot of bone, and dust. He is at the point where time devours its own tail and no longer means anything. If he has information for the passerby, it is not to be defined and not to be escaped. His stiff fingers, each showing a single nailed joint —

except for the right index which has dropped a joint among the bandages — are laid on a quivering nerve of the human animal, which no education, no reason, no faith, can entirely still. If children are not hurried past by their parents, they look, and ask urgent questions. Then comes the crunch, and parents fight a rear-guard action with the example of cut hair and nails and a reminder of heaven. But he is more immediate than heaven; and after a child has studied the gaunt effigy and the silent wooden box with its staring eyes, there is nothing more to be said — no defence against the new half-knowledge that will lend to a grandfather clock or a tall cupboard a subsidiary suggestion their makers never intended.

The mummy lies there, then; and we cannot feel in our bones that it is just a thing, nor that it is indifferent. The hollow eye-sockets with their horn-like lids drawn a little apart, the stick-thin neck, the broken cheek that allows us a glimpse of the roots of teeth, have a kind of still terror about them. It is eternally urgent, as inevitably to be inspected as air is to be breathed. So as I leave my showcase — and the only sound is a door shutting where an attendant prepares to turn the hush into a vigil — I keep the showcase between me and him, then circle, facing him always, till I stand where I can see the naked bones of his head. He excites, moves, disgusts, absorbs. He is a dead body but on permissive show behind glass. So I stand, watching him; and I do not credit him with my humanity. I do something far more mysterious and perhaps dangerous. I credit myself with his. He is part of the whole man, of what we are. There is awe and terror about us, ugliness, pathos, and this finality which we cannot believe is indifference, but more like a preoccupation.

We are mysterious ourselves. Else, why was I so desperate, so frightened and so determined? Why did my will produce the next step and reveal to me my own complexity? For one day, when I was about ten, and leaning over a showcase as usual, I found a man at my side. He said 'Excuse me, sonny.' He moved me away from the case and opened it with a key. I watched him with respect for he was a curator. He was one with my heroes, Schliemann, Pitt-Rivers, and Flinders-Petrie, men I believed in touch with levels and explanations that would have surprised them had they known. In some sense, this curator had the hot sand, the molten sun of Egypt lying in his turnups. I felt his tweedy jacket had been windblown on a dozen sites. He was big. Was he not what I wanted to become? His face was a little fat, and reddened. There was a ring of sandy curls round the baldness of his head. He was a cheerful man, as I soon discovered, whistling in the hush as if it were not sacred, but so habitual as to be unnoticed. He hummed sometimes to himself, as he arranged the amulets in a pattern which pleased him better. He took notice of me, questioned me, and soon found out that I was as learned an Egyptologist as I could well be, considering my age. At last he asked me — who desired nothing better — if I would like to give him a hand with some work he had to do. We went together through a museum I already felt to be more personally mine, I in the shorts, jersey, socks and shoes of an English schoolboy, he in his tweedy jacket and baggy flannels. We passed out of the Egyptian department, through the hall devoted to relics of the Industrial Revolution, through another hall full of stuffed animals, and up wide, marble stairs to the geological department. One corner of the room had been partitioned off from the rest. There was no ceiling to this part, as I discovered when the curator opened the door with another key and I followed him in. It was a makeshift division in what had once been a room of a splendid and princely house.

But it was a division full of significance. There were rows of green filing cabinets, with papers sticking out of the drawers. There were shelves of books, proceedings of learned societies, and other expensive volumes that I had heard of but could not afford. Lying open on a desk was the British Museum facsimile of the Book of the Dead in all its rich colour. Wherever I looked, things added up into an image of the life I guessed at but had not known, the world of the wise men, the archaeologists. There was a diorite vase, surely from the depths of the Step Pyramid; there was a Greek dish, from Alexandria, perhaps, but most scandalously misused, since I saw a fat roll of cigarette ash in it, and a curl of half-burnt paper. There were predynastic flint knives, and in one corner of the room a broken, sandstone altar, its scooped out channels waiting patiently for blood.

But all these, which I took in at a glance, were nothing to the main exhibits. A sarcophagus, tilted like a packing case, leaned against the left-hand wall. The lid leaned against the wall alongside it, inner surface revealing a white painting of Nut the

Sky Goddess. I could see how the lid had been anthropo-
morphized, indicating by its curves the swelling of hips and
chest, the neat hair, the feet. But the painted face was hidden in
shadow, and stared away from us at the wall. Nor did I try long
to see the face, because the lid and the box were no more than a
preliminary. Before me, only a foot or two away on a trestle
table, head back, arms crossed, lay a wrapped and bandaged
mummy.

There was a new kind of atmosphere, some different quality
in the space between me and it, because no glass kept me away.
Glass multiplies space, and things in glass cases have an
illogical quality of remoteness. I was not prepared for this
difference; and I was not prepared for the curator's casual
habitual approach. He stood on the other side of the mummy,
hands resting on the table and looked at me cheerfully.

'You can give me a hand with this, if you like.'

I could have shaken my head, but I nodded, for my fate was
on me. I guess that my eyes were big, and my mouth pinched a
little. Yet at the same time there was an excitement in me that
was either a part of, or at war with — I am not certain which —
my awe and natural distaste for the object. If I have to define my
state of mind I should say it consisted in a rapid oscillation
between unusual extremes; and this oscillation made me a little
unsteady on my feet, a little unsure of the length of my legs;
and like a ground bass to all this turmoil was the knowledge
that by my approach, by my complicity, by the touch which must
surely take place of my hand on the dead, dry skin, I was storing
up a terrible succession of endless dark nights for myself.

But he had commenced without waiting for more than a nod
from me. He was untying the long bandages that harnessed in
the first shroud. As they came free, he handed them to me and
told me to roll them up and put them on the side table. He
hefted the thing itself and it turned on the table like another
piece of wood. It was much harder inside the bandages and
shrouds than you might suppose, turning with a sort of dull
knock. He took off the outer shroud a large oblong of linen, now
dark brown, which we folded, the two of us, as you might fold a
bedsheet — he, holding one end for a moment with his chin. I
knew what we should look for next. Each limb, each digit, was
wrapped separately, and the amulets to ensure eternal security

77

and happiness were hidden among the bandages. Presently they appeared one by one as we took the bandages away — little shapes of blue faience. It seemed to me in my wider oscillation, my swifter transition from hot to cold, that they were still warm from the hands of the embalmer/priest who was the last to touch them three thousand years ago, and who was surely standing with us now, whenever now was. But our operations had their own inevitability; and at last I laid my compelled, my quivering and sacrilegious hand on the thing in itself, experienced beyond all Kantian question, the bone, and its binding of thick, leathery skin.

The curator glanced at his wristwatch and whistled, but with astonishment, this time.

'I've kept you late, sonny. You'd better go straight away. Apologise to your parents for me. You can come back tomorrow, if you like.'

I left him standing alone or partly alone, where I knew I should never dare to stand myself. The face of the sarcophagus was still hidden against the wall, but the curator was smiling at me out of his round, red face, under a fringe of curly hair. He waved one hand, and there was a hank of browning bandage in it, above a brightly lit and eternally uncheerful grin. I hurried away through the deserted museum with my contaminated hands to the dark streets and the long trek home. There I told my parents and my brother in excited detail about what had happened, was cross questioned, and finally prepared for the terrors of bed.

Now it is important to realize that I remembered and still remember everything in vivid and luminous detail. It became the event of my life; and before I returned to the museum, I talked the thing over passionately, with my parents and myself. I suffered the terrors of bed. I wrote an essay describing the episode when I went to school, and got extravagant praise for it. I brooded constantly about the lid of the sarcophagus with its hidden face. Yet it is important to realize that none of the episode happened at all. From the moment when I stood by the showcase, brooding and desperate, wishing, as singlemindedly as the hero of a fairy tale, till the time when I ran helter-skelter down the museum steps, I was somewhere; and I still do not know where that was. There was no curator with a red, smiling face. There was no mummy, and no sarcophagus. There was a partitioned corner of the geological room, but it contained rolls of maps, not bandages. I looked at the place in daylight and knew myself to be a liar, though I do not think now that a liar is exactly what I was. It was the childish equivalent of the Lost Weekend, the indulgence behind which was my unchildish learning, and my overwhelming need to come to terms with the Egyptian thing. The whole self-supplying episode is a brilliant part of the Egypt from my inside; stands with all the other pictures, the black and gold figures at the final entrance to Tutankhamen's tomb, the Hall of Pillars at Karnak, and all the vignettes, fantastic, obscure, meaningful, that illustrate the Book of the Dead.

But the episode resolved nothing, only made the need bleaker and more urgent. I took my desperation down from the daylight of the geological department and the rolls of maps, and stood once more by the showcase in the Egyptian room, where there was a mummy and no curator to open the lid and rearrange the amulets. All day I wandered, brooding and drawing. As night fell I knew there was still one thing to do. For the face that did not exist on the lid of the sarcophagus that did not exist had been turned to the wall and I had never seen it. But there was a 'real' sarcophagus in the Egyptian collection. It stood on its feet behind glass by the wall. It looked across the room. It was nearly seven feet tall; and however I moved about the room among the showcases it gazed fixedly over my head.

There is nothing quite so real as the eyes of a primitive carving. Everything else may be rough-hewn, approximate or formalized. Indeed, the eyes may be formalized too, but if so, all they exaggerate is the stare. I know that it is necessary to meet that stare, eye to eye. It is a portrait of the man himself as his friends thought he should be — purified, secure, wise. It is the face prepared to penetrate mysteries, to stand pure and unfrightened in the hall where the forty-two judges ask their questions of the dead man, and the god weighs his heart against a feather. It is the face prepared to go down and through, in darkness. I too can go down and through, I can revisit the man with his red face and fringe of hair. I can comprehend and control the silent mummy by meeting those eyes, and understanding them, outstaring them. I go to the opposite wall, though it means being near the wrecked, dead thing. I get one foot on the valve of a radiator and lift myself perhaps eight or nine inches into the air but it is not enough. The mummiform sarcophagus with its carved and painted face still stares over my head as if there were a picture above me on the blank wall. I get down from the radiator and carry a chair from the door, but carefully; for who knows what might move, at a sudden noise? I am trembling, and every now and then, this trembling is interrupted by a kind of convulsive shudder. My teeth are gripped and I am at my apex. I put the chair soundlessly by the wall and climb up, then turn to look across the nearer, bandaged thing to the massive, upright figure. I am at eye-level with the awful, the pure face before its judges; but it does not see me nor a picture on the wall. Those formalized black and white oblongs focus where parallel lines meet. They outstare infinity in eternity. The wood is rounded as in life, but not my life, insecure, vulnerable. It dwells with a darkness that is its light. It will not look at me, so frightened yet desperate. I try to force the eyes into mine; but know that if the eyes focused or I could understand the focus, I should know what it knows; and I should be dead. On my chair I search for the unattainable focus of its vision in growing fear, until there is nothing but shadows round and under the staring oblongs which have detached themselves and swim unsupported. I scramble down, go quickly and silently away through the halls where the Chinese idols and the eyeslitted suits of armour are friendly, normal things; and outside the revolving doors there are red buses, and wintry-breathing people, and cars.

It will be observed that I do not understand these transactions; which is as much as to say that though I can describe the quality of living I do not understand the nature of this being alive. We are near the heart of my Egypt. It is to be at once alive and dead; to suggest mysteries with no solution, to mix the strange, the gruesome and the beautiful; to use all the resources of life to ensure that this leftover from living and its container shall stand outside change and bring the wheel to a full stop.

'The Egyptians', we are assured, 'were a laughter- and life-loving people. They were earthy. We meet them only in their coffins and get their lives out of proportion.' It may be so; yet for all their life- and laughter-love, that *is* where we meet them.

That is what they made of themselves and I cannot see how we are to escape it. Whatever the Egyptians intended, they brought life and death together in the most tangible way possible. Their funerary rituals, their tombs and grave goods, their portrait statues on which no human eye was supposed to rest, their gloomy corridors irradiated with paint, their bones, skin and preservatives — these are not just a *memento mori*. They are a *momento vivere* as well. I recognize in their relics, through the medium of archaeology and art, my own mournful staring into the darkness, my own savage grasp on life. I have said how familiar to me their bad art is. When a shoddy ship model confronts me, with the scale all wrong and the figures no more lifelike than a clothespeg, I am at home in daylight; for it is the sort of model I might make myself. But their great art, I cannot understand, only wonder at a wordless communication. It is not merely the size, the weight, the skill, the integrity. It is the ponderous movement forward on one line which is none the less a floating motionlessness. It is the vision. Beyond the reach of the dull method, of statistical investigation, it is the thumbprint of a mystery.

We are not, for all our knowledge, in a much different position from the Egyptian one. Our medicine is better, our art, probably not so good; and we suffer from a dangerous pride in our ant-like persistence in building a pyramid of information. It is entertaining information for the most part, but it does not answer any of the questions the Egyptians asked themselves before us. And we have a blinding pride that was foreign to them. We discount the possibility of the potentialities of the human spirit which may operate by other means in other modes to other ends. For if we or the Egyptians confine ourselves to the accepted potential, the limits are plain to see. For them perhaps, it was those four pillars, the arms and legs of Nut, the Sky Goddess, beyond which investigation was useless. For us, the limit is where the receding galaxies move with the speed of light beyond all possibility of physical investigation. Yet in their effect on us and in their relationship to those other guessed-at qualities of the human spirit, they are the same limits.

Well. Most of us today are children of Herodotus. But though I admire the Greeks I am not one of them, nor one of their intellectual children. I cannot believe as the sillier of my ancestors did, that the measurements of the great pyramid give us the date of the next war, nor that pounded mummy flesh makes a medicine, yet my link with the Egyptians is deep and sure. I do not believe them either wise or foolish. I am, in fact, an Ancient Egyptian, with all their unreason, spiritual pragmatism and capacity for ambiguous belief. And if you protest on the evidence of statistical enquiry they were not like that, I can only answer in the jargon of my generation, that for me they have projected that image.

BOOKS

Fable

'N uncle,' says the fool in Lear, 'thou hast pared thy wit o'
both sides and left nothing i' the middle. Look — here
comes one of the parings.' The paring in question is
Goneril and she gives him a dirty look. No one has ever been
quite sure what happened to the fool later on. He disappears
halfway through the play in mysterious circumstances, but we
need not be surprised. He asked time and again for summary
measures to be taken against him. Oh, the uncomfortable
counsel he gave! 'Thou did'st little good when thou mad'st thy
daughters thy mothers.' He tries to comfort Lear; to turn his
mind from his sorrows; but ever and again the bitter truth will
out. Notice that he never says 'It was a piece of folly to put
yourself in the power of your bloody-minded daughters'.
Always the truth is metaphorical. So he disappears; and though
Shakespeare nowhere says so, it is plain enough to me that Lear's
daughters got him in the end. For the fool was a fabulist, and
fabulists are never popular. They are those people who haunt the
fringes of history and appear in miscellanies of anecdotes as slaves
or jesters, rash courtiers, or just plain wise men. They tell the
dictator, the absolute monarch what he ought to know but does
not want to hear. Generally they are hanged, or beheaded or even
bow-stringed, unless they have the wit to get out of that hole
with another pretty jest. It is a thankless task, to be a fabulist.

Why this is so is clear enough. The fabulist is a moralist. He
cannot make a story without a human lesson tucked away in it.
Arranging his signs as he does, he reaches, not profundity on
many levels, but what you would expect from signs, that is
overt significance. By the nature of his craft then, the fabulist is
didactic, desires to inculcate a moral lesson. People do not much
like moral lessons. The pill has to be sugared, has to be witty
or entertaining, or engaging in some way or another. Also, the

85

moralist has to be out of his victim's reach, when the full impact of the lesson strikes him. For the moralist has made an unforgiveable assumption; namely that he knows better than his reader; nor does a good intention save him. If the pill is not sufficiently sugared it will not be swallowed. If the moral is terrible enough he will be regarded as inhuman; and if the edge of his parable cuts deeply enough, he will be crucified.

Any of Aesop's fables will do as examples to begin with. The fox who loses his tail in a trap and then tries to persuade all the other foxes to cut theirs off, because a fox looks better that way, is a situation that may be paralleled in human experience easily enough. But, you cannot make a scale model. This is why *Animal Farm*, George Orwell's splendid fable, having to choose between falsifying the human situation and falsifying the nature of animals, chooses to do the latter. Often, we forget they are animals. They are people, and Orwell's brilliant mechanics have placed them in a situation where he can underline every moral point he cares to make. We read his funny, poignant book and consent to the lesson as much out of our own experience as out of his. There are fables from other centuries, *Gulliver's Travels*, *Pilgrim's Progress*, perhaps *Robinson Crusoe*. Children love them, since by a God-given urgency for pleasure, they duck the morals and enjoy the story. But children do not like *Animal Farm*. Why should the poor animals suffer so? Why should even animal life be without point or hope? Perhaps in the twentieth century, the sort of fables we must construct are not for children on any level.

With all its drawbacks and difficulties, it was this method of presenting the truth as I saw it in fable form which I adopted for the first of my novels which ever got published. The overall intention may be stated simply enough. Before the second world war I believed in the perfectibility of social man; that a correct structure of society would produce goodwill; and that therefore you could remove all social ills by a reorganization of society. It is possible that today I believe something of the same again; but after the war I did not because I was unable to. I had discovered what one man could do to another. I am not talking of one man killing another with a gun, or dropping a bomb on him or blowing him up or torpedoing him. I am thinking of the vileness beyond all words that went on, year after year, in the totalitarian states. It is bad enough to say that so many Jews were exterminated in this way and that, so many people liquidated — lovely, elegant word — but there were things done during that period from which I still have to avert my mind less I should be physically sick. They were not done by the headhunters of New Guinea, or by some primitive tribe in the Amazon. They were done, skilfully, coldly, by educated men, doctors, lawyers, by men with a tradition of civilization behind them, to beings of their own kind. I do not want to elaborate this. I would like to pass on; but I must say that anyone who moved through those years without understanding that man produces evil as a bee produces honey, must have been blind or wrong in the head. Let me take a parallel from a social situation. We are commonly dressed, and commonly behave as if we had no genitalia. Taboos and prohibitions have grown up round that very necessary part of the human anatomy. But in sickness, the whole structure of man must be exhibited to the doctor. When the occasion is important enough, we admit to what we have. It seems to me that in nineteenth-century and early twentieth-century society of the West, similar taboos grew up round the nature of man. He was supposed not to have in him, the sad fact of his own cruelty and lust. When these capacities emerged into action they were thought aberrant. Social systems, political systems were composed, detached from the real nature of man. They were what one might call political symphonies. They would perfect most men, and at the least, reduce aberrance.

Why, then, have they never worked? How did the idealist concepts of primitive socialism turn at last into Stalinism? How could the political and philosophical idealism of Germany produce as its ultimate fruit, the rule of Adolf Hitler? My own conviction grew that what had happened was that men were putting the cart before the horse. They were looking at the system rather than the people. It seemed to me that man's capacity for greed, his innate cruelty and selfishness, was being hidden behind a kind of pair of political pants. I believed then, that man was sick — not exceptional man, but average man. I believed that the condition of man was to be a morally diseased creation and that the best job I could do at the time was to trace the connection between his diseased nature and the international mess he gets himself into.

BOOKS

To many of you, this will seem trite, obvious and familiar in theological terms. Man is a fallen being. He is gripped by original sin. His nature is sinful and his state perilous. I accept the theology and admit the triteness; but what is trite is true; and a truism can become more than a truism when it is a belief passionately held. I looked round me for some convenient form in which this thesis might be worked out, and found it in the play of children. I was well situated for this, since at this time I was teaching them. Moreover, I am a son, brother, and father. I have lived for many years with small boys, and understand and know them with awful precision. I decided to take the literary convention of boys on an island, only make them real boys instead of paper cutouts with no life in them; and try to show how the shape of the society they evolved would be conditioned by their diseased, their fallen nature.

It is worth looking for a moment at the great original of boys on an island. This is *The Coral Island*, published a century ago, at the height of Victorian smugness, ignorance, and prosperity. I can do no better than quote to you Professor Carl Niemeyer's sketch of this book.

'Ballantyne shipwrecks his three boys — Jack, eighteen; Ralph, the narrator, aged fifteen; and Peterkin Gay, a comic sort of boy, aged thirteen — somewhere in the South Seas on an uninhabited coral island. Jack is a natural leader, but both Ralph and Peterkin have abilities valuable for survival. Jack has the most common sense and foresight, but Peterkin turns out to be a skilful killer of pigs and Ralph, when later in the book he is separated from his friends and alone on a schooner, coolly navigates back to Coral Island by dead reckoning, a feat sufficiently impressive, if not quite equal to captain Bligh's. The boys' life on the island is idyllic; and they are themselves without malice or wickedness, tho' there are a few curious episodes in which Ballantyne seems to hint at something he himself understands as little as do his characters.... Ballantyne's book raises the problem of evil — which comes to the boys not from within themselves but from the outside world. Tropical nature to be sure, is kind, but the men of this non-Christian world are bad. For example the island is visited by savage cannibals, one canoeful pursuing another, who fight a cruel and bloody battle, observed by the horrified boys and then go away. A little later, the island is again visited, this time by pirates (i.e. white men who have renounced or scorned their Christian heritage) who succeed in capturing Ralph. In due time the pirates are deservedly destroyed, and in the final episode of the book the natives undergo an unmotivated conversion to Christianity, which effects a total change in their nature just in time to rescue the boys from their clutches.

'Thus Ballantyne's view of man is seen to be optimistic, like his view of English boys' pluck and resourcefulness, which subdues tropical islands as triumphantly as England imposes empire and religion on lawless breeds of men.'

Ballantyne's island was a nineteenth-century island inhabited by English boys; mine was to be a twentieth-century island inhabited by English boys. I can say here in America what I should not like to say at home; which is that I condemn and detest my country's faults precisely because I am so proud of her many virtues. One of our faults is to believe that evil is somewhere else and inherent in another nation. My book was to say: you think that now the war is over and an evil thing destroyed, you are safe because you are naturally kind and decent. But I know why the thing rose in Germany. I know it could happen in any country. It could happen here.

So the boys try to construct a civilization on the island; but it breaks down in blood and terror because the boys are suffering from the terrible disease of being human.

The protagonist was Ralph, the average, rather more than average, man of goodwill and commonsense; the man who makes mistakes because he simply does not understand at first the nature of the disease from which they all suffer. The boys find an earthly paradise, a world, in fact like our world, of boundless wealth, beauty and resource. The boys were below the age of overt sex, for I did not want to complicate the issue with that relative triviality. They did not have to fight for survival, for I did not want a Marxist exegesis. If disaster came, it was not to come through the exploitation of one class by another. It was to rise, simply and solely out of the nature of the brute. The overall picture was to be the tragic lesson that the English have had to learn over a period of one hundred years; that one lot of people is inherently like any other lot of people; and that the only enemy of man is inside him. So the picture I had in my mind of the change to be brought about was exemplified by two pictures of the little boy Ralph. The first is when he discovers he is on a real desert island and delights in the discovery.

'He jumped down from the terrace. The sand was thick over his black shoes and the heat hit him. He became conscious of the weight of clothes, kicked his shoes off fiercely and ripped off each stocking with its elastic garter in a single movement. Then he leapt back on the terrace, pulled off his shirt, and stood there among the skull-like coco-nuts with green shadows from the palms and the forest sliding over his skin. He undid the snake-clasp of his belt, lugged off his shorts and pants, and stood there naked, looking at the dazzling beach and the water.

'He was old enough, twelve years and a few months, to have lost the prominent tummy of childhood; and not yet old enough for adolescence to have made him awkward. You could see now that he might make a boxer, as far as width and heaviness of shoulders went, but there was a mildness about his mouth and eyes that proclaimed no devil. He patted the palm trunk softly; and, forced at last to believe in the reality of the island, laughed delightedly again, and stood on his head. He turned neatly on to his feet, jumped down to the beach, knelt and swept a double armful of sand into a pile against his chest. Then he sat back and looked at the water with bright, excited eyes.'

This is innocence and hope; but the picture changes and the book is so designed that our last view of Ralph is very different. By the end, he has come to understand the fallen nature of man, and that what stands between him and happiness comes from inside him; a trite lesson as I have said; but one which I believed needed urgently to be driven home.

Yet if one takes the whole of the human condition as background of a fable it becomes hopelessly complex, tho' I worked the book out in detail.

Let us take, for example, the word 'history'. It seems to me that the word has two common meanings, each of them of awful importance. First there is what might be called academic, or if you like campus history. To my mind this is not only of importance, but of supreme importance. It is that objective yet devoted stare with which humanity observes its own past; and in that stare, that attempt to see how things have become what they are, where they went wrong, and where right, that our only hope lies of having some control over our own future. The exploration of the physical world is an art, with all the attendant aesthetic pleasures; but the knowledge we get from it is not immediately applicable to the problems that we have on hand. But history is a kind of selfknowledge, and it may be with care that selfknowledge will be sufficient to give us the right clue to our behaviour in the future. I say a clue; for we stand today in the same general condition as we have always stood, under sentence of death.

But there is another kind of force which we call history; and how uncontrollable that force is even in the most detached of men was amusingly demonstrated to me only the other day. I was being driven over the last battleground of the War Between the States, a historical episode which I am able to observe with some objectivity. My driver was a southerner and scholar. His exposition to me of the situation was a model of historical balance. He explained to me how the south had embarked on a war which they could not hope to win, in support of a pattern of society which could not hope to survive. He was perhaps a little harder on the south than a northerner would have been; but judicially so. As the day wore on, his voice began to return to its origins. Emotion crept in — not very far, because of course he was a scholar, and scholars are detached and unemotional are they not? — At a discreet forty miles an hour we followed the wavering fortunes of battle down into Virginia. Here, he told me, Lee had performed that last incredible tactical feat in the defence of Richmond; here, Grant had sidestepped — but what was this? His voice had lost all pretence of scholarship. Insensibly the speed of the car had increased. When we came to Appomattox, this educated and indeed rather cynical man grunted — 'Aw, shucks!' and drove past the place where Lee surrendered to Grant at seventy-five miles an hour.

This is a different force from campus history. It is history felt in the blood and bones. Sometimes it is dignified by a pretty name, but I am not sure in my own mind that it is ever anything but pernicious. However this is a political and historical question which we need not settle here and now. My point is that however pathetic or amusing we find these lesser manifestations of prejudice, when they go beyond a certain point no one in the world can doubt that they are wholly evil. Jew and Arab in the name of religion, Jew and Nordic in the name of race, Negro and white in the name of God knows what.

And it is not only these larger more spectacular examples of frozen history which do the damage. I am a European and an optimist. But I do not believe that history is only a nominal thing. There have been many years when as I contemplate our national frontiers, I have fallen into something like despair. Frontiers in Europe may be likened to wrinkles in an aged face, and all that will remove them is the death of the body. Now I know you will point out to me that Europe is already moving towards some confederation; and I would agree and add that that confederation has the full support of every man of goodwill and commonsense. But the wrinkles are so deep. And I cannot think of a confederation in history where the members voluntarily bowed to supranational authority without at least one of the members fighting a war to contest it. In Europe there is and has been a terrible fund of national illwill, handed down from generation to generation. There are habits of feeling which have acquired the force of instinct. These habits of feeling may be encouraged in school or college, but they are rarely taught there. They are an unconscious legacy wished on children by their parents. A woman, like one old French lady I knew, who had gone through the business of being conquered three times, in 1870, 1914 and 1940, had acquired an attitude to the Germans which was a hate so deep that she shook when she thought of them. Indeed, as I make these words, I am aware in myself of resents, indignations and perhaps fears which have nothing to do with today, with the England and Germany of today, in a word, with reality, but are there, nevertheless. I got them from off-campus history; and unless I make a conscious effort I shall hand them on. These impulses, prejudices, even perhaps these *just* hates which are nevertheless backward-looking are what parents luxuriating in a cheap emotion can wish on their children without being properly conscious of it and so perpetuate division through the generations. A less painful example of this is the way in which where one Englishman and one American are gathered together, that sad old story of the eighteenth century will raise its head, so that the American whose ancestors have perhaps been in the States since 1911 will be arrogating to himself all the splendours of that struggle, while the Englishman who may have spent his life in the pursuit and furtherance of liberal principles may find himself forced into the ridiculous position of defending his fellow Englishman George III. My own technique on these occasions is to start talking about the vicious occupation of my country by the Romans and the splendid resistance to them by our own heroes, Queen Boadicea and King Arthur. Some of these examples are silly, meant to be silly, and are understood as silly by the contestants. They are less severe than the partisanship roused by games of one sort or another; nevertheless they are symptomatic. We ought not to underestimate the power or the destructiveness of these emotions. The one country to leave the British Commonwealth of Nations in recent centuries is the Union of South Africa, forced out by a universal, if sometimes smug condemnation of her policy towards her own black population. But a quarter of a century ago England and Australia were shaken to the very roots of their common interests by a game of cricket. Those of you who find this incredible either do not understand the tenuousness of the bond that holds Australia and England together, or else do not understand the fierce passions that can be roused by cricket. But the point is that many Englishmen and Australians did in fact begin to think of each other as objectionable, irrational, ill-disposed, vindictive. For a moment each nation, or at least the sillier members of each — and there are always enough silly people in any country to form a sizeable mass-movement — each nation stood squarely behind their culture heroes, the one a very fast and accurate bowler, the other a batsman who objected to being struck repeatedly on the head. If the random agglomeration of nations which is the commonwealth seems to you to have any power for good, you may consider it lucky that England and Australia are twelve thousand miles apart. Had they been separated, not by half a world, but by a relatively small ocean, Australia might have taken her bat and gone off fiercely to play cricket by herself. It was George Orwell who commented on the destructive force of international contests. Anyone who has watched a television programme of a game between two European nations must agree with him. There's savagery for you. There's bloodlust. There's ugly nationalism raising its gorgon head.

What I am trying to do is to add together those elements, some horrible, some merely funny, but all significant, which I suppose to be the forces of off-campus history. They are a failure of human sympathy, ignorance of facts, the objectivizing of our own inadequacies so as to make a scapegoat. At moments of optimism I have felt that education and perhaps a miracle or two would be sufficient to remove their more dangerous elements. When I feel pessimistic, then they seem to constitute a trap into which humanity has got itself with a dreary inevitability much as the dinosaur trapped itself in its own useless armour. For if humanity has a future on this planet of a hundred million years, it is unthinkable that it should spend those aeons in a ferment of national self-satisfaction and chauvinistic idiocies. I was feeling pessimistic when I tried to include a sign for this thing in a fable.

The point about off-campus history is that it is always dead. It is a cloak of national prestige which the uneducated pull round their shoulders to keep off the wind of personal self-knowledge. It is a dead thing handed on, but dead though it is, it will not lie down. It is a monstrous creature descending to us from our ancestors, producing nothing but disunity, chaos. War and disorder prolong in it the ghastly and ironic semblance of life. All the marching and countermarching, the flags, the heroism and cruelty are galvanic twitches induced in its slaves and subjects by that hideous, parody thing. When I constructed a sign for it, therefore, it had to be something that was dead but had a kind of life. It had to be presented to my island of children by the world of grownups. There was only one way in which I could do this. First I must take the children at a moment when mature council and authority might have saved them as on so many occasions we might have saved our own children, might have been saved ourselves. Since a novelist ought not preach overtly in a fable, the situation had to be highlighted by the children having some dim knowledge that wisdom, that commonsense even, is to be found in the world of grownups. They must yearn for it, now they have begun to find the inadequacy of their own powers. I took a moment therefore, when they had tried to hold a council meeting to discuss ways and means but had found that other questions came up — questions which they would sooner have ignored. Finally the meeting breaks down. The children who are retrogressing more rapidly have gone off into the wardance with which they fortify their own sense of power and togetherness. It is dark. The few remainder, puzzled, anxious, surrounded by half perceived threats and mysteries; faced with a problem which once looked so simple of solution, the maintenance of a fire on the mountain, but which proved to be too much for them — these few, men of goodwill, are searching for some hope, some power for good, some commonsense.

'If only they could get a message to us', cried Ralph desperately. 'If only they could send us something grown-up . . . a sign or something.'

What the grown-ups send them is indeed a sign, a sign to fit into the fable; but in the fable sense, that arbitrary sign stands for off-campus history, the thing which threatens every child everywhere, the history of blood and intolerance, of ignorance and prejudice, the thing which is dead but won't lie down.

'There was no light left save that of the stars. The three bigger boys went together to the next shelter. They lay restlessly and noisily among the dry leaves, watching the patch of stars that was the opening towards the lagoon. Sometimes a little 'un cried out from the other shelters and once a big 'un spoke in the dark. Then they too fell asleep.

'A sliver of moon rose over the horizon, hardly large enough to make a path of light even when it sat right down on the water; but there were other lights in the sky, that moved fast, winked, or went out, though not even a faint popping came down from the battle fought at ten miles' height. But a sign came down from the world of grown-ups, though at that time there was no child awake to read it. There was a sudden bright explosion and a corkscrew trail across the sky; then darkness again and stars. There was a speck above the island, a figure dropping swiftly beneath a parachute, a figure that hung with dangling limbs. The changing winds of various altitudes took the figure where they would. Then, three miles up, the wind steadied and bore it in a descending curve round the sky and swept it in a great slant across the reef and the lagoon towards the mountain. The figure fell and crumpled among the blue flowers of the mountain-side, but now there was a gentle breeze at this height too and the parachute flopped and banged and pulled. So the figure, with feet that dragged behind it, slid up the mountain. Yard by yard, puff by puff, the breeze hauled the figure through the blue flowers, over the boulders and red stones, till it lay huddled among the shattered rocks of the mountain-top. Here the breeze was fitful and allowed the strings of the parachute to tangle and festoon; and the figure sat, its helmeted head between its knees, held by a complication of lines. When the breeze blew the lines would strain taut and some accident of this pull lifted the head and chest upright so that the figure seemed to peer across the brow of the mountain. Then, each time the wind dropped, the lines would slacken and the figure bow forward again, sinking its head between its knees. So as the stars moved across the sky, the figure sat on the mountain-top and bowed and sank and bowed again.'

I have no time to prolong this quotation, nor is it necessary, since I am glad to say the book itself remains in print. But it is perhaps worth noticing that this figure which is dead but won't lie down, falls on the very place where the children are making their one constructive attempt to get themselves helped. It dominates the mountaintop and so prevents them keeping a fire alight there as a signal. To take an actual historical example, the fire is perhaps like the long defunct but once much hoped-over League of Nations. That great effort at international sanity fell before the pressures of nationalism which were founded in ignorance, jealousy, greed — before the pressures of off-campus history which was dead but would not lie down.

Having got thus far, I must admit to a number of qualifications, not in the theory itself but in the result. Fable, as a method, depends on two things neither of which can be relied on. First the writer has to have a coherent picture of the subject; but if he takes the whole human condition as his subject, his picture is likely to get a little dim at the edges. Next a fable can only be taken as far as the parable, the parallel is exact; and these literary parallels between the fable and the underlying life do not extend to infinity. It is not just that a small scale model cannot be exact in every detail. It is because every sort of life, once referred to, brings up associations of its own within its own limits which may have no significant relationships with the matter under consideration. Thus, the fable is most successful *qua* fable when it works within strict limits. George Orwell's *Animal Farm* confines itself to consideration and satire of a given political situation. In other words, the fable must be under strict control. Yet it is at this very point that the imagination can get out of hand.

I had better explain that I am not referring now to normal exercises of imagination, which we are told is the selection and rearrangement of pictures already latent in the mind. There is another possible experience, which some may think admirable and others pathological. I remember, many years ago, trying to bore a hole with a drilling machine through armour plate. Armour plate is constructed to resist just such an operation — a point which had escaped me for the time being. In my extreme ignorance, I put the drill in the chuck, held by half an inch of its extreme end. I seized the handle and brought the revolving drill down on the armour. It wobbled for a second; then there was a sharp explosion, the drill departed in every direction, breaking two windows and taking a piece of my uniform with it. Wiser now, I held the next drill deep in the chuck so that only the point protruded, held it mercilessly in those steel jaws and brought it down on the armour with the power behind it of many hundred horses. This operation was successful. I made a small red-hot hole in the armour, though of course I ruined the drill. If this small anecdote seems fatuous, I assure you that it is the best image I know for one sort of imaginative process. There is the same merciless concentration, the same will, the same apparently impenetrable target, the same pressure applied steadily to one small point. It is not a normal mode of life; or we should find ourselves posting mail in mailboxes which were not there. But it happens sometimes and it works. The point of the fable under imaginative consideration does not become more real than the real world, it shoves the real world on one side. The author becomes a spectator, appalled or delighted, but a spectator. At this moment, how can he be sure that he is keeping a relationship between the fable and the moralized world, when he is only conscious of one of them? I believe he cannot be sure. This experience, excellent for the novel which does not claim to be a parable must surely lead to a distortion of the fable. Yet is it not the experience which we expect and hope the novelist to have?

It might be appropriate now to give an example of a situation in which something like this happened. For reasons it is not necessary to specify, I included a Christ-figure in my fable. This is the little boy Simon, solitary, stammering, a lover of mankind, a visionary, who reaches commonsense attitudes not by reason but by intuition. Of all the boys, he is the only one who feels the need to be alone and goes every now and then into the bushes. Since this book is one that is highly and diversely explicable, you would not believe the various interpretations that have been given of Simon's going into the bushes. But go he does, and prays, as the child Jean Vianney would go, and some other saints — though not many. He is really turning a part of the jungle into a church, not a physical one, perhaps, but a spiritual one. Here there is a scene, when civilization has already begun to break down under the combined pressures of boy-nature and the thing still ducking and bowing on the mountaintop, when the hunters bring before him, without knowing he is there, their false god, the pig's head on a stick. It was at this point of imaginative concentration that I found that the pig's head knew Simon was there. In fact the Pig's head delivered something very like a sermon to the boy; the pig's head spoke. I know because I heard it.

'You are a silly little boy,' said the Lord of the Flies, 'just an ignorant, silly little boy.'

Simon moved his swollen tongue but said nothing.

'Don't you agree?' said the Lord of the Flies. 'Aren't you just a silly little boy?' Simon answered him in the same silent voice.

'Well then,' said the Lord of the Flies, 'you'd better run off and play with the others. They think you're batty. You don't want Ralph to think you're batty, do you? You like Ralph a lot, don't you? And Piggy, and Jack?'

Simon's head was tilted slightly up. His eyes could not break away and the Lord of the Flies hung in space before him.

'What are you doing out here all alone? Aren't you afraid of me?'

Simon shook.

'There isn't anyone to help you. Only me. And I'm the Beast.'

Simon's mouth laboured, brought forth audible words.

'Pig's head on a stick.'

'Fancy thinking the Beast was something you could hunt and kill!' said the head. For a moment or two the forest and all the other dimly appreciated places echoed with the parody of laughter. 'You knew, didn't you? I'm part of you? Close, close,

close! I'm the reason why it's no go? Why things are what they are?'

The laughter shivered again.

'Come now', said the Lord of the Flies. 'Get back to the others and we'll forget the whole thing.'

Simon's head wobbled. His eyes were half-closed as though he were imitating the obscene thing on the stick. He knew that one of his times was coming on. The Lord of the Flies was expanding like a balloon.

'This is ridiculous. You know perfectly well you'll only meet me down there — so don't try to escape!'

Simon's body was arched and stiff. The Lord of the Flies spoke in the voice of a schoolmaster.

'This has gone quite far enough. My poor, misguided child, do you think you know better than I do?'

There was a pause.

'I'm warning you. I'm going to get waxy. D'you see? You're not wanted. Understand? We are going to have fun on this island. Understand? We are going to have fun on this island! So don't try it on, my poor misguided boy, or else —'

Simon found he was looking into a vast mouth. There was blackness within, a blackness that spread.

'— Or else,' said the Lord of the Flies, 'we shall do you. See? Jack and Roger and Maurice and Robert and Bill and Piggy and Ralph. Do you. See?'

Simon was inside the mouth. He fell down and lost consciousness.

That then is an example of how a fable when it is extended to novel length can bid fair to get out of hand. Fortunately the Lord of the Flies' theology and mine were sufficiently alike to conceal the fact that I was writing at his dictation. I don't think the fable ever got right out of hand; but there are many places I am sure where the fable splits at the seams and I would like to think that if this is so, the splits do not rise from ineptitude or deficiency but from a plenitude of imagination. Faults of excess seem to me more forgivable than faults of coldness, at least in the exercise of craftsmanship.

And then I remind myself that after all, the last lecture on sign, symbol, fable and myth, and this one more particularly on fable, are exercises not in craftsmanship but in analysis. I suspect that art, like experience, is a continuum and if we try to take elements out of that continuum, they cease to be what they were, because they are no longer together. Take these words, then, as efforts to indicate trends and possibilities rather than discrete things. May it not be that at the very moments when I felt the fable to come to its own life before me it may in fact have become something more valuable, so that where I thought it was failing, it was really succeeding? I leave that consideration to the many learned and devoted persons who, in speech and the printed word, have explained to me what the story means. For I have shifted somewhat from the position I held when I wrote the book. I no longer believe that the author has a sort of *patria potestas* over his brainchildren. Once they are printed they have reached their majority and the author has no more authority over them, knows no more about them, perhaps knows less about them than the critic who comes fresh to them, and sees them not as the author hoped they would be, but as what they are.

At least the fable has caught attention, and gone out into the world. The effect on me has been diverse and not wholly satisfactory. On the good side it has brought me here, seven thousand miles from home, jet-propelled tho' somewhat jaundiced. It has subjected me to a steady stream of letters. I get letters from schoolmasters who want permission to turn the book into a play so that their classes can act it. I get letters from schoolmasters telling me that they *have* turned the book into a play so that their classes can act it. Now and again I get letters from mothers of boys whose schoolmasters have turned the book into a play so that their classes can act it. I get letters from psychiatrists, psychologists, clergymen — complimentary, I am glad to say; but sometimes tinged with a faint air of indignation that I should seem to know something about human nature without being officially qualified.

And at the last — students. How am I to put this gently and politely? In the first place, I am moved and fulfilled by the fact that anyone of your generation should think a book I have written is significant for you. But this is the standard form of the letters I get from most English speaking parts of the world.

Dear Mr. Golding, I and my friend so and so have read your book *Lord of the Flies* and we think so forth and so forth.

However there are some things in it which we are not able to understand. We shall be glad therefore if you will kindly answer the following forty-one questions. A prompt reply would oblige as exams start next week.

Well there it is. I cannot do your homework for you; and it is in some ways a melancholy thought that I have become a school textbook before I am properly dead and buried. To go on being a schoolmaster so that I should have time to write novels was a tactic I employed in the struggle of life. But life, clever life, has got back at me. My first novel ensured that I should be treated for the rest of my days as a schoolmaster only given a longer tether — one that has stretched seven thousand miles.

In My Ark

I remember walking in a steep Welsh valley and turning aside
to see if the nuts were ripe. I lifted a leaf and found it covered
a red squirrel about the length of my thumb. He held a nut in
his forepaws, and in proportion it was much larger than a
rugby football. We looked at each other for perhaps half a
minute in mutual astonishment; then he dropped the nut and
left. I remember, off Cape Trafalgar, watching the dolphins
outspeeding us at twenty-eight knots. The sea was alive with
them, leaping and turning from horizon to horizon. I remember
watching migrant starlings coming in over the downs, a
gossamer, a scarf, then a whole sky-concealing blanket and a
tempest of song. They dropped on part of Savernake forest and
the bare trees seemed to be covered at once with an abundant
and noisy foliage. I remember these things as any man would;
but I do not love squirrels or dolphins or starlings. I am glad
they are there, more or less, but I do not dwell on them. Dogs
bore me and I view our present national devotion to the horse
with an indifference tempered by the reflection that it is a
curious love of horses which gelds them, breaks them in, loads
them with harness, dumps a human weight on their backs and
sets them at the jumps of the Grand National or the cross-
country course of the Olympic Games. I can only suppose that a
sufficiently profound telepathic sense has discovered that the
horses like it.

I feel myself more attuned to a certain placid agriculturalist.
He received a command out of the blue to build a boat. He was
no boat-builder but he did as he was told. Then, as if that were
not enough, he was told — though he was no zoologist either —
to take two of every animal and give them freight space. He did
not love animals. His heart was in viticulture. The vine stays in
one place and does not scream when you prune it. But, again, he

set to. When he made his farmer's landfall, hard and fast aground on the top of a mountain, he turned the animals loose with an unrecorded but inevitable relief, and neither he nor his descendants took any further notice of them. He had done his duty. He was not asked to love them, to distinguish between the itsy-bitsy furry things, the cuddly-wuddlies, the nasty creatures that refuse to be tamed and useful, or the splendid stallions saying 'Ha! Ha!' He merely ensured the continuance of the lot as far as he could, because he was told to, out of the blue. They did not belong to him. They belonged to Adam; but that was in Paradise. Adam was found unworthy to own them, as we might do well to remember.

I would preserve a dinosaur in my ark if I could, but not out of affection. Our manipulation of the world has grown explosive. Animals are capital, but they are not ours. I do not know whose they are, nor whose we are, except that we do not belong to ourselves. Once in a way, I smell purpose in the world and guess it may include not only Adam but also the delectable lamb and the loathsome spider.

So the positive *love* of animals has always amazed me. I had told myself that these lovers must be persons of superabundant affections, who, having exhausted the possibilities of loving their own species, have enough left for the brute creation. In fact I had supposed them Franciscan. It was only another proof, I thought, of my own inadequacy as a person that I should find a human family and friends and certain others to be more than sufficient objects for my own affections. Dogs would find an arid space round my feet.

But now Gavin Maxwell has blown the gaff. In his latest book,[1] he confesses honestly that he prefers animals to human beings. He would be a willing Noah, passionately collecting his pairs, but regarding Shem, Ham and Japheth as little more than cage-cleaners or hands for working ship. This put me out of sympathy with his book, or at best made me read it as the record of an aberration which I would try to understand. And I was curious, because rumour of his otters had reached me from one source and another.

Let me say at once that *The Ring of Bright Water* is an excellent and most individual book. Only about half of it is concerned

[1] *The Ring of Bright Water*, by Gavin Maxwell.

with otters; and Maxwell's deep involvement in their lives catches at the reader whether he is familiar with animals or not. One shares a passionate sorrow at the death of Mijbil even while finding it excessive: one is glad at the extraordinary chain of events which brought Edal to take Mijbil's place. But beyond that this reader, at any rate, cannot go. A man's bed seems a preposterous place for an otter; and Maxwell's positive servitude to an otter's comfort and safety is humiliating in some curious way. It is the human obverse of that other unnatural world, the world of performing elephants and fleas, in which animals do grotesquely what they should never be asked to do at all. An otter bitch — if that is the right term — should be introduced to a dog otter and given the liberty of a river. They are not, as Mr. C. S. Lewis would say, they are not 'Hnau'. They do not lie awake all night and weep for their sins; and perhaps they have the best of it. Let them be.

The book itself divides into halves. It is partly about otters and partly about a place; and when Gavin Maxwell occupies himself with the hills and the waterfall and beach of Camusfeárna his book becomes engrossing and magnificent. His prose, overcharged at times, is nevertheless a fit vehicle for the individual nature of his seeing. Details are held and focused close to the eye in a way which is at once poetic and childlike — or perhaps the one because the other. He is a traveller who has made himself a permanent home, a place of return on the remote western shores of Scotland. There is only one cottage within miles. The sea and mountains, the seals and stags, the wild cats and mackerel are his more immediate neighbours. What is so splendid about this book is the way in which he has actualized for us not only the bare bones of the place but its very atmosphere, the immediacy of a nature which today is only too seldom untouched. We understand how he lives as a man among real things, how he allows them their impact, strips the labels from them, does not confine them by preconceptions or dreary systems.

For the ring of bright water is many things. It is the astonishingly colourful stretch of water inside the Hebrides; and then again it may be the pock and spreading circle where a fish has leapt or a heron stood. But more than this, it chimes with river Ocean which circled the known world, home, as the Gnostics thought, of mysterious spirits and unfathomable secrets of creation. Maxwell has the great gift of intransigence in the face of popular belief. He recognizes mystery and he values it, as any man must whose mind has not come to a full stop.

'There is perpetual mystery and excitement in living on the seashore, which is in part a return to childhood and in part because for all of us the sea's edge remains the edge of the unknown; the child sees the bright shells, the vivid weeds and red sea-anemones of the rock pools with wonder and with a child's eye for minutiae; the adult who retains wonder brings to his gaze some partial knowledge which can but increase it, and he brings, too, the eye of association and of symbolism, so that at the edge of the ocean he stands at the brink of his own unconscious.'

We stand, then, on the shore, not as our Victorian fathers stood, lassoing phenomena with Latin names, listing, docketing and systematizing. Belsen and Hiroshima have gone some way towards teaching us humility. We would take help and a clue from anywhere we could. It is not the complete specimen for the collector's cabinet that excites us. It is the fragment, the hint. For the universe has blown wide open, is a door from which man does not know whether blessing or menace will come. We pore, therefore, over the natural language of nature, the limy worm-casts in a shell, 'strange hieroglyphics that even in their simplest form may appear urgently significant, the symbols of some forgotten alphabet, the appearance of Hindoo temple carving, or of Rodin's Gates of Hell, precise in every riotous ramification.' We walk among the layers of disintegrating coral, along the straggling line of 'brown sea-wrack, dizzy with jumping sand hoppers'. We stand among the flotsam, the odd shoes and tins, hot-water bottles and skulls of sheep or deer. We know nothing. We look daily at the appalling mystery of plain stuff. We stand where any upright food-gatherer has stood, on the edge of our own unconscious, and hope, perhaps, for the terror and excitement of the print of a single foot.

Islands

It is always interesting to revisit the scenes of our childhood, and literary scenes have the endearing property of changelessness. No ribbon building or estate development obscures the view. The old scenes are there, exactly the same as they were, waiting for us between the covers of a book. I have just been encouraged to do some revisiting by the arrival on my desk of *The Swiss Family Robinson* and *Treasure Island* in an agreeable format and a large type which is easy on the adult eye.

What a pair of books! Has anyone ever resisted the charm of the Swiss Family? Indeed, can anyone think of it as just another book? Someone once likened Chaucer's stories to an English river, slow, quietly beautiful, and winding all the way. In the same terms, *The Swiss Family Robinson* is like a mountain lake. It is contained and motionless. It does not go anywhere. It has no story. Details, and detached incidents, are looked at separately without regard to what is coming next. This is how children live when they are happy, and this is why children will read *The Swiss Family Robinson* backwards and forwards and not bother about the end. To the adult eye, very little seems intended for out-and-out realism. When father Robinson puts together his boat of tubs with the ease and speed of a Popeye who has just eaten spinach, we, and children too, accept a literary convention. Nor are the vague people at all convincing. For Johann Wyss began, not by writing for a wide public but for his children who knew him and his wife and themselves too well to bother about characterization, even if he had been capable of it. Having isolated his characters, Wyss used the book from then onwards as a sort of holdall for conveying moral instruction and scientific information. He did not foresee the outcome of the book. One feels that the lively and capable Miss Montrose was brought in at the end because Wyss's eldest son had got engaged and Wyss wanted to bring his fiancée into the family. The charm of the book, then, lies precisely in the absence of story. The days are endless and time has no meaning. We sink completely into the milieu of these people who are not going anywhere and do not mind. Time is bright and uncomplicated as holidays spent by the sea in childhood.

At the back of the book stands the determination of Wyss to make and keep his family secure. How safe the Swiss Family Robinson is! That omniscient and omnipotent father, God's representative on earth to his family; that mild, womanly and devoted mother who is nevertheless so competent in her defined sphere — there is no hint that they can be anything but perfect. There is no flaw in their parental authority. This makes it disconcerting, in the new illustrated edition, to find father Robinson red-headed, and a fit hero for a Western, while Mother is a slim and beautiful girl, only a year or two older than her eldest child. I can't help feeling, if the illustrations are anything to go by, that *this time* family life may not be so uncomplicated and placid.

In the text, as ever, the children take a child's place. There is simply no possibility of juvenile delinquency. The guiding hand is gentle but adamant. The children are not allowed to over-shadow their parents and save the day, perhaps because these are not the sort of days that have to be saved. We should no more expect Fritz to succour his father and mother than we should expect Jim Hawkins, conversely, to stay in the stockade and allow Doctor Livesey to take top place. It may be that the convention of children knowing more than their parents, being heroic and returning to a saved and admiring father, was a reaction against that gentle but adamantine hand. You can have too much of a good thing after all; and sometimes even a child's eye detects the absurdities in that godlike father-figure.

But no one, either child or adult, laughs at Johann Wyss without affection. He achieved more than he hoped or imagined possible. He gave his own family, and a good slice of European youth, total security between the covers of a book. For the great strength of *The Swiss Family Robinson* is not the brilliantly evoked spirit of place (the crystal cavern, the lobster pools, the grove of trees); it is not even the details held up to the eye and exactly observed (the tools and weapons, the plants and rocks, the good, earned meals). What Wyss captured effortlessly because it was so familiar to him was that family sense — the period when children are no longer babies and not yet young men: the period when a family, if it is lucky and emotionally stable, can look in on itself and be a whole world.

When one turns to *Treasure Island*, one sees immediately that Stevenson was the professional, knowing precisely what effects he wanted and how he was going to get them. Every chapter is shaped and fitted into the general structure like the timbers of a ship. There are moments of lambent actuality which only come to a writer at full, dedicated stretch. Who can forget the notch in the sign of the Admiral Benbow, or the musket shot that spat like a curse through the mainsail of the departing ship?

Treasure Island was written to order and is deliberately sub-adolescent. 'No women', stipulated the boy for whom it was written; and perhaps significantly, there is no father either. Feminine interest is limited to Jim's Mum, who is allowed a little hand-wringing, some tremulous greed, and a splendid faint. Clearly she is not intended for the larger air, and the poor woman is nicely tidied up in the first few chapters. From then on, it is salt water and cutlasses all the way.

So much praise has been poured out on *Treasure Island* that I tried to find something to carp at; and found precious little. The book remains sharp and swift as I remember it. Surprisingly enough, however, since I left the nursery and went to sea myself, the topsail-schooner *Hispaniola* — an unusual rig for the eighteenth century — has become a little fuzzy round the edges. This is a pity, as she used to be my favourite ship. Stevenson chose her because he thought himself unable to handle square-rig; but she never lies before us in one convincing piece. Her tonnage remains in doubt. She was big enough to carry thirty people or more to the Pacific. We have Captain Smollett's own word for it that she was splendid at sea; she 'lay a point closer to the wind than a man has a right to expect of his own wife'. Yet later he anchors her in nine feet of water.

A small, frivolous point, that one. But dare I say, in the teeth of the applauding generations, that I do not find *Treasure Island*, the physical patch of land itself, wholly in focus? We get glimpses that are superb; that sandy gash with the two-guinea piece lying in the middle of it where the treasure had been, the fort and stockade, the glade where Silver murdered Tom so horribly. But the island as it stuck out of the sea, the reason for it being there, and the relationship between the parts, escapes me even when I used the overrated chart. An island must be built, and have an organic structure, like a tooth.

There my carping ends. It was 'Q' who first showed the craftsmanship of the construction, and how each episode is contributory yet dramatically complete. I can find no better example than his. See how Stevenson takes Jim out in the coracle, puts him aboard the masterless schooner, embroils him with Israel Hands, gets him chased to the crosstrees, and ends the episode with a mighty climax :

'I was drinking in his words and smiling away, as conceited as a cock on a wall, when, all in a breath, back went his right hand over his shoulder. Something sang like an arrow through the air; I felt a blow and then a sharp pang, and there I was pinned by the shoulder to the mast. In the horrid pain and surprise of the moment — I scarce can say it was by my own volition, and I am sure it was without conscious aim — both my pistols went off, and both escaped from my hands. They did not fall alone; with a choked cry, the cockswain loosed his grasp on the shrouds, and plunged headfirst into the water.'

Characterization remains vivid. The bluff and unsubtle Squire Trelawney, forthright and minatory Captain Smollett, mature Doctor Livesey, honest Redruth and feckless Ben Gunn — they all stand up to close examination. Even the remainder are not without substance. They were, I should think, fugitives from the disbanded Hawkhurst Gang. Their talk strikes the perfect middle way between the literal and the emasculated.

'I saw him dead with these here deadlights', said Morgan. 'Billy took me in. There he laid with penny pieces on his eyes.'

'Dead — aye, sure enough he's dead and gone below', said the fellow with the bandage; 'but if ever sperrit walked, it would be Flint's. Dear Heart, but he died bad, did Flint!'

'Aye, that he did', observed another; 'now he raged, and now he hollered for the rum, and now he sang. "Fifteen men" were his only song, mates, and I tell you true I never rightly like to hear it since. It was main hot, and the windy was open, and I hear that old song comin' out as clear as clear — and the death-haul on the man already.'

But the lifeblood of the book is Long John Silver. Most writers can invent a Baddy, and a few of them a Goody. But there are some characters in books who live their own abundant life beyond the threshold of our business of moral judgments. Here we are, they seem to say, and now what are you going to make of us? Despite their authors they are outside good and evil. They exist by right of their own joy in life. They are as naturally and brilliantly alive as a swallow diving on a cat. Who can doubt that Silver enjoys his villainy, likes to be liked, finds success and failure a huge joke? For the other mutineers are small-time crooks, doomed from the beginning. But Silver disappears at the end with a modest competence, to start all over again. He goes, having delighted in the murders, the turning of coats, the devious treacheries. When he vanishes from our sight in port, good and evil have become irrelevant standards of judgment. One can almost hear him quoting from another book as he goes — 'What larks, Pip, eh? What larks!'

Astronaut by Gaslight

A child's ignorant eye can make a Western out of a Dumas tapestry. Many of us can remember the quality of the Western:

'I will reward you, my dear, by passing that time with you, which I intended to pass with your mistress.'

The years have taught us that D'Artagnan did not pass the time in showing Kitty those tricks of fence with which he and/or Douglas Fairbanks was able to pink a brace of opponents. As for La Vallière, Buckingham and the Queen, as for the ladders and trapdoors, the assignations and *billets-doux*, the hissing, tittering complications — I, personally, am stunned when I think what a passionless pattern I made of it all. If we revisit our childhood's reading, we are likely to discover that we missed the satire of *Gulliver*, the evangelism of *Pilgrim's Progress*, and the loneliness of *Robinson Crusoe*.

But when we revisit some books in this way, we find that the iridescent film has burst, to leave nothing behind but a wet mark. Henty, Ballantyne, Burroughs, require an innocence of approach which, while it is natural enough to a child, would be a mark of puerility in an adult. I declare this with some feeling, since during the last week or so I have undertaken a long course of Jules Verne, and suffer at the moment, not from indigestion so much as hunger.

Yet once these books[1] satisfied me. They held me rapt, I dived with the *Nautilus*, was shot round the moon, crossed Darkest Africa in a balloon, descended to the centre of the earth, drifted in the South Atlantic, dying of thirst, and tasted — oh rapture! It always sent me indoors for a drink — the fresh waters of the Amazon. And now?

[1] *Journey to the Centre of the Earth, 20,000 Leagues Under the Sea, From the Earth to the Moon, Round the Moon, Five Weeks in a Balloon, At the North Pole, The Wilderness of Ice* and *Propellor Island*.

Books

Of course the books have not vanished wholly. They have the saving grace of gusto. Verne had his generation's appetite for facts, and he serves them up in *grande cuisine*: 'How amazing . . . were the microscopical jellyfish observed by Scoresby in the Greenland seas, which he estimated at 23,898,000,000,000,000,000 in an area of two square miles!' But a diet of such creatures palls, for Verne's verbal surface lacks the slickness of the professional; it is turgid and slack by turns. Only the brio of his enthusiasm carries us forward from one adventure to another. What is left for the adult is off-beat; something so specialized that to enjoy it is about as eccentric as collecting the vocal chords of prima donnas. For Verne attracts today, not so much by his adventures as by the charm of his nineteenth-century interiors. The lamplight lies cosily on thick curtains and elaborate tables. Clubs are as rich and secure as an Egyptian tomb. They have no servant problem, the carpets are never worn, and the subscription will never go up. Here live the savants, and a savant is related to a scientist as an antiquary is to an archaeologist. He is a learned enthusiast, a man of boundless absurdity, energy and stubbornness. At any moment he may leap from his hip-bath, sell his Consols and buy 1,866 gallons of sulphuric acid, 16,050 pounds of iron and 11,600 square feet of twilled Lyons silk coated with gutta-percha. His oath is 'A thousand thunders!' Cross him, and he will dash his smoking-cap into the grate. Take leave to doubt his wisdom and he will attempt to assault you. Held back by force, he will wager a fortune on the outcome of his adventure. Without knowing it, he passes a large part of his life under the influence of alcohol, for at the touch of success he will dash off, or drain off, or toss off, a bumper of brandy, which he follows with an endless succession of toasts. This half-gallon or so of brandy has as little effect on him as whisky has on the tough hero of a television serial. Indeed, his euphoria has always been indistinguishable from intoxication. Champollion is his ancestor in the real world, and Conan Doyle's professor in *The Lost World* his literary descendant.

This typification is moderated but not destroyed by national distinction. Verne reserved, as was perhaps natural, his greatest *élan* for the French, or at least, the Europeans. He divided sang-froid between the English and the American. All these qualities, and others, are laid on with the trowel of farce. Indeed, the sang-froid of his Englishman, Mr. Phineas Fogg, is at times indistinguishable from advanced schizophrenia. But when his characters let themselves go — here is Captain Nemo expressing his sense of displeasure:

'Captain Nemo was before me but I could hardly recognize him. His face was transfigured. His eyes flashed sullenly; his teeth were set; his taut body, clenched fists, and head hunched between his shoulders, betrayed the violent agitation that pervaded his whole frame. He did not move. My telescope, fallen from his hands, had rolled at his feet.'

I must remember that these jerky cut-outs once convinced me, moved me, excited me, as they still move children. They fit our picture of the nineteenth century. What about the Marquis of Anglesey and the Duke of Wellington at Waterloo?

'By G—d Sir, I have lost my leg.'

'By G—d Sir, so you have.' If that had not been a real exchange, Verne would have invented it.

What the child misses most in these books — if I am anything to go by — is the fact that Verne was a heavy-handed satirist. The organization which fires its shot at the moon is the Gun Club of Boston. These were the savants who engaged in the arms race of the American Civil War.

'Their military weapons attained colossal proportions, and their projectiles, exceeding the prescribed limits, unfortunately occasionally cut in two some unoffending bystanders. These inventions, in fact, left far in the rear the timid instruments of European artillery.'

After that we are not surprised to learn that the honour accorded to the members of the Gun Club was 'proportional to the masses of their guns, and in the direct ratio of the square of the distances attained by their projectiles.' Their personal appearance is at once ludicrous and horrifying:

'Crutches, wooden legs, artificial arms, steel hooks, caoutchouc jaws, silver craniums, platinum noses, were all to be found; and it was calculated by the great statistician Pitcairn that throughout the Gun Club there was not quite one arm between four persons, and exactly two legs between six. Nevertheless, these valiant artillerists took no particular account of these little facts, and felt justly proud when the dispatches of a battle returned the number of victims at tenfold the quantity of the projectiles expended.'

Throughout the seventeen books there is an almost total absence of women. Verne was honester here than some of his SF descendants who lug in a blonde for the look of the thing. His male world was probably all he could manage. You cannot hack out a woman's face with an axe; he could not, or would not, write about women. He remains the only French writer who could get his hero right round the world without meeting more than one woman while he was doing it.

Verne's talent was not spurred by a love of what we should now call pure science, but by technology. His books are the imaginative counterpart of the Great Eastern, the Tay Bridge, or the Great Steam Flying Machine. It is this which accounts for his continued appeal to sub-adolescent boyhood. For the science sides of our schools are crammed to bursting with boys who have confused a genial enjoyment in watching wheels go round with the pursuit of knowledge. His heroes, too, are a pattern of what the twelve-year-old boy considers a proper adult pattern — they are tough, sexless, casually brave, resourceful, and *making something big*. Compared with the Sheriff of Dumb Valley, or the Private Eye, they constitute no mean ideal; to the adult, their appeal is wholly nostalgic. Apart from the odd touch that convinces — the pleasures of Professor Aronnax when, after years of groping for fish, he observes them through the windows of *Nautilus;* the willingness of the Frenchman to go to the moon with no prospect of coming back — apart from this they are a dead loss.

A study of Verne makes me uncomfortable. It seems that on the level of engineering, predictions can be made that will come true. So the soberer SF is no more than a blueprint for tomorrow. In time we can expect to see photographs — TV programmes — of acrobats performing on the moon, beneath the blue domes of Lunarville. The hot-spot which lies near the gantries of Marsport, that sleazy cantonment peopled with whisky-slinging space pilots and interplanetary whores, is a fact of the twenty-first century. This prospect would not dismay me, had one of Verne's characters not suggested that the heating of a colossal boiler to three million degrees would one day destroy the world.

Nevertheless, Verne's nineteenth-century technology and

mania for size sometimes result in a combination which has a charm to be found nowhere else. He was excited with arc lighting and gives us a picture with all the fascination of an early lantern slide. Light itself, sheer brilliance, is an enchantment to him, when it is produced by man. In *The Wilderness of Ice*, we can share a forgotten moment. Today, the light of an atomic explosion is a savage thing which blinds and burns. We have gone as far as our eyes can go. If we want to discover a new quality in light, we have to return to the pit lamp, or candle. But to Verne, the white-hot carbon was a near-miracle :

'Then two pieces of carbon rod, placed in the lantern at the proper distance, were gradually brought closer together, and an intense light, which the wind could not dim nor diminish, sprang from the lantern. It was marvellous to see these rays, whose glory rivalled the whiteness of the [snowy] plain, and which made all the projections round it visible by their shadow.'

Perhaps the best moment comes when we get a mixture of the fantastic, but future and possible, with the ordinary paraphernalia of nineteenth-century living. In *Round the Moon*, the three voyagers move about their spaceship, peering delightedly at this and that. In the shadow of the earth all is dark; but as they move into the sun's rays, they find them shining *up* through the base of the ship — and are able to turn off the light, in order to save gas.

Lastly I must mention a splendid picture from the original edition of this book, which the publishers, to their great credit, have preserved for posterity. It is a, or rather *the*, moment of free fall — not the modern sort which can be endless, but the nineteenth-century sort, the point where earth and moon gravity is equal. The three voyagers, dressed as for a stroll in the park *circa* 1860, are helpless in the air, as are the dog and the two hens. A telescope and top hat hang near them. The walls of the spaceship are padded, but the padding has the effect of ornate wallpaper. The three gentlemen, a little startled, but not distressingly so, hang over their shadows. Softly, the gaslight pours down.

Headmasters

Those who are wary of Lytton Strachey but flinch from engaging with Stanley's thick volumes will be grateful to Mr. Bamford for presenting this new study of Thomas Arnold.[1] He does so with a detachment which is judicious but cold; and indeed a personality does not emerge very sharply from these pages. Arnold's swarthy and passionate face looks out past us from the dust-cover; not the face of a myth, one would say. Yet that portrait, typical of its period, tells us a great deal. We examine the doctor's robes, the clergyman's bands, the sumptuous volume on the knees. These and the waxen, lay-figure hands, which support rather than grasp the open volume, might be expected. But the face is a different matter. Here is energy, impatience and self-esteem. Here is a man who bounced into the studio. Where shall I sit? How? How long? I haven't much time. Is that right? I am engaged in a most important matter that simply *must*. . . .

And surely he was off again before he had done more than leave an image on the artist's retina? The waxen hands, the robes, the bands remain; but surely the face had to be a snapshot, rapid movement arrested in flight? It is an impetuous and choleric face. Such a man would not be content to *hold* opinions. He would squeeze them, he would almost throttle them. He might achieve a great thing; but so much speed and energy would leave his back unguarded, where ridicule lies in wait.

Thomas Arnold was a boy of the middle class who, at the age of nineteen, got a First in Greats, won the English Prize Essay, and was made a Fellow of Oriel. The paper work of his examination for the fellowship was not outstanding. Nor were his family connections, good though some of them might be, sufficiently brilliant to ensure him the benefits of nepotism.

[1] *Thomas Arnold*, by T. W. Bamford.

What won him his fellowship was an air of nascent authority which impressed all who knew him. Neither he nor they knew what he would do, but he would do something. At the age of nineteen he was *capax imperii*. At twenty-one he was awarded the Chancellor's Latin Prize. At twenty-three, after a drawn battle over the Thirty-nine Articles, he was ordained in the Church of England. His rise seemed inevitable. He would be head of a college, perhaps — certainly a bishop. The Province of Canterbury was not out of reach.

Yet Arnold gave up his fellowship and became a schoolmaster. It is astonishing but true to say that Arnold moved or drifted into teaching for the commonest reason of all; he wanted to get married. He never thought of teaching as a permanency. He was a reformer in the wide world. He sought to bring about 'an inequality where some have all the enjoyments of civilized life and none are without its comforts — where some have all the treasures of knowledge and none are sunk in ignorance. That is a social system in harmony with the order of God's creation in the natural world.'

To this end he was dedicated. But teaching would do as a temporary measure. It would tide him over until better things appeared. He felt no vocation for it. But he was Thomas Arnold. He did the job with passion even though it was not the centre of his interests.

The key to Arnold's nature, at every level, seems to have been passion. He was a reformer who did not so much approach a problem as declare personal war on it. At first his ideas on Church Reform, radical though they were, gained him a good deal of respect. But he attacked the High Church wing in the person of Newman so ferociously that he lost it again. And disquieting things were happening at the school. *Capax imperii.* The board who appointed him Headmaster of Rugby at the age of thirty-one must have wondered whether the other half of the tag, *nisi imperasset*, might not have something for Arnold as well.

For what is a headmaster? Is he a leader? A co-ordinator? Is he to be a dictator, or a constitutional monarch? There is no post of responsibility in which a man is left so free to choose his own method. He may choose a cloistered virtue and live for the school. But the occupational hazard in this sort of life is grandiosity. He meets parents, masters, and boys. But boys lack the experience and audacity to challenge him; masters lack the energy to engage; and parents have given hostages to fortune. As for that freer audience, the governors, a self-regarding instinct will not readily allow them to question the wisdom of their own choice. A headmaster who begins by dedicating himself wholly to this closed community may end in the placid admiration of his own image.

It need not be so. There have been many headmasters who, in the words of the Tory press,
'sought their reward, not in the applause of publications relating to the passing events of the day, but in the genius, the acquirements and the success of their pupils. They held it beneath their dignity to become political partisans.'
Arnold might have chosen to be one of these; but he did not do so. He remained in two worlds, so that the school, always distinguished, now became the centre of a political storm. He preached his Christian Radicalism to the sixth form. Stanley's parents knew what was happening.

'Arthur was a running commentary upon Arnold's Church Reform — knowing so well what he meant by this, what led him to that, and recognizing his illustrations and references.'

Since the name of 'Radical' was attached to Arnold, much as the name of 'Communist' might be attached to a headmaster today, the propaganda offered to his captive audience made him the Bad Man of the Tory press. His denunciation of Newman — not yet gone over to Rome — left the Right wing outraged: 'in all the annals of the worst times of Popery [can] any anathema be found breathing a spirit of malevolence worse than this?' At that time, Arnold was on the short list for a mitre. Lord Melbourne was the arbiter. It is a quaint comment on the organization of a State Church that we hear, through all the lofty sentiments that surrounded the question of appointing bishops, the strong, clear call of the party politician. 'What have the Tory churchmen ever done for me that I should make them a present of such a handle against my government?' The sensitive hand that held a mitre, paused, and took it back again.

Yet the question of Arnold's methods — his tempestuous kidnapping of the soul — goes far beyond party politics. It raises a fundamental issue in the ethics of responsibility, and Mr. Bamford is right to dwell on it. The Arnold sort of headmaster brings his grandiosity, his overpowering *rightness*, with him. The majesty of the great world lies round his shoulders like a cloak. Boys find him irresistible.

Newman went over to Rome and took others with him. Public opinion veered towards Arnold : he was right after all. They made him Regius Professor of History at Oxford, a post he could hold at the same time as his headmastership. The mitre hovered near again. Then, at the age of forty-seven, with the same precipitancy that had characterized all his actions — almost with the same urgency and passion — he died.

Arnold, famous in his life as a reformer, has become a totem of the Victorian public school system. Yet he disapproved of public schools. They took children away from their parents and the boys corrupted each other. What mattered was a sixth form which he could mould as he wished. The sixth form was an *élite* on which he lavished his learning and his passion, and to which he gave an authority that was absolute. They were to be made in his own image — reformers of a turbulent and misguided society. He was successful : for while boys will always listen to masters more than they pretend, they will listen without reservation to a master who has made some mark in the outside world. And what a mark Arnold had made! He was treated by one half of the press as a monster and idolized by the other. He was tomorrow's bishop or archbishop. He was a man of superb assurance who gave you faith in yourself so long as you went the way he wanted.

Is it any wonder he was successful with the sixth form? They took him neat. It is often said that Arnold the headmaster must be judged by the best of his pupils. Clough and Stanley, his most brilliant creations, remained what he made them. Clough perhaps, had doubts.

'[Arnold] used to attack offences, not as offences — the right view — against discipline, but as sins, heinous guilt, I don't know what beside! Why didn't he flog them and hold his tongue? Flog them he did, but why preach?'

But Stanley remained what he was made till his dying day; and Stanley was to be Arnold's most influential biographer.

That is the danger of the Arnold system. It implies that one man can know exactly what another ought to be. So that when his admirers silence criticism by pointing to his pupils, Clough,

Vaughan, Stanley, they raise a question which sounds so indecent that it is never asked. Let us ask it, then. Would you like to be Clough or Stanley? Would you give yourself up to a kind of jesuitical moulding process which is all the more powerful because you are not old enough to understand it? Moreover, Arnold has laid the way open for lesser men who imitated him to create the smug, the self-righteous prigs who regard themselves as a chosen people because some local boss of a closed shop has consistently told them they were so. Arnold knew the will of God. His sense of rightness led him into cruelty and dishonesty. One of his first actions as headmaster was to beat a small boy who appeared to lie. A little deliberation would have saved them both, but the awful immorality of a lie brought the blood into those swarthy cheeks. The boy had told the truth. Then again Rugby was a foundation for the education of local children. Arnold killed the lower school, to keep them out; and in so doing prised open the gap that still lies between the public schools and the rest. Though what he did was illegal and immoral, he knew he was right, and he was unperturbed. God believed in a stratified society.

One is haunted throughout Mr. Bamford's careful book by the knowledge that Arnold was to exercise a wide influence over Victorian education, and so on to our own times. Generations of boys have grown up by Arnold out of Stanley. Yet neither of them, Dean or Professor of History, guessed how the future would shape. If you have an empire, you have to have the men to run it. Arnold's Rugby became the pattern for a hundred new foundations which saw their first duty in a steady stream of trained and pruned young men to take law to the black, brown and yellow. At his best, then, and at second hand, he may be said to have produced the men and the tradition which made such a shining example of the administration of the Sudan. At his worst, he made certain the pattern of colonialism which gave a convulsive shudder in the tragedy of Suez.

Tolstoy's Mountain

A few weeks ago I said goodbye to a friend of mine who was going off to climb a mountain. He had graduated by way of cliffs, fells and Welsh mountains to the Alps; and now he proposed to climb the Matterhorn. I wished him success with the thankful feeling that all such adventures were a long way behind me. But the very next morning there was delivered to my door a parcel, not so much wrapped as boxed — not a carton so much as a packing case. I opened it, lugged the contents into my study and dumped it on my desk. It was a new, illustrated, one-volume edition of *War and Peace*.[1]

Well, I ask you! What can one say? This is a *massif central*, not to be climbed without guides, ropes, ice-axes and, for me at least, an attendant helicopter. Moreover, despite its international reputation, its universal appeals, it is a Russian mountain, superficially as remote as the Tien Shan. My difficulties begin at the most frivolous level. Like the generality of dull people, I find the very names confusing. I have passport trouble.

Another and greater difficulty is the translation. Whatever Constance Garnett's competence as a Slavonic scholar, I am not convinced that what I read was what Tolstoy intended. The effect that the verbal surface brings me is one of vagueness and imprecision. Time and again I caught myself thinking that what people were saying was slightly off balance, slightly obscured, just beside the point. When Beckett and Pinter do this, however they may puzzle me, I accept the intention immediately because they are writing in their own tongue. But all the time in *War and Peace* I was aware that I did not entirely understand the implications and overtones, was ignorant of the assumptions that a native Russian would make without knowing he was making

[1] *War and Peace*, by Leo Tolstoy. Illustrated by John Groth.

them. I felt the need of some such assurance as you used to get in German editions of Aristophanes — an asterisk and a footnote to the effect that the author has made a joke. I do not know how I should distribute the blame for this vagueness between Tolstoy, Constance Garnett and my own ignorance. I cannot even get some sort of fix by cross-bearings from my copy of Leo Wiener's translation. His is a spikier text, certainly, but no more convincing.

Nevertheless, the mountain emerges. It is covered in cloud which passes continually, without allowing more than glimpses of separate features, so that the shape of the whole remains in doubt. But this, after all, is a recommendation, another way of saying the mountain is too vast for photography, but can be explored endlessly. *War and Peace* has this in common with the works of Shakespeare and Homer. You can go on discussing the book for the rest of your life. This may not be an official measuring rod in criticism, but it is a very real one.

Peering, remembering, I ask myself what the book is about. Death? Birth? Love? Purpose? Causality? The nature of reality? History? War? Many years ago, when I first read this book, I was inclined to think that it was about the nature of war. But today I would at least qualify that assertion by saying that it is about the Napoleonic Wars and no other. Presumably Tolstoy thought he was making statements that were true for all time, but, if so, he was wrong. War had suffered dialectical changes before his time and has gone on changing since. I do not mean that war has increased out of all recognition in its power of destruction. Men have always had it in their power to destroy their *known* world. War has changed, above all, in the degree to which the director knows what is going on and in his capacity to control it.

Tolstoy was very likely right in his picture of a Napoleon who knew little and controlled nothing once battle was inevitable. Battles on land and sea were fought in anæsthetizing fogs of gunsmoke where communication was impossible. But since then, the fog of war has thinned. Between 1940 and 1945, battles were fought on the map. Napoleon, receiving information which was both inaccurate and out-of-date, could do nothing but send a message which would arrive long after the supposed need for it had lapsed through changing circumstances. Montgomery at

Alamein could switch his armour from one sector to another on reliable information and at his personal decision. Whole invasions were conducted to a timetable, with moves planned and carried out as in chess. Whatever we pawns may have thought about it, directors of the game could give battles a formal beauty which looks very well on paper. The Napoleonic, or Tolstoyan, mode of war, therefore — its aimlessness and the consequent need for soldiers and historians to invent a pattern that never existed — is a piece of dead history, as irrelevant to the twentieth century as the stage-coach. Great Men, in that aimlessness, that absence of communications, controlled nothing. They were catalysts in a way that neither Tolstoy nor anyone else has ever been able to understand. But an increase in the means of communication is an increase in the powers of individual persuasion and command. It brings back the Great Man. Big Brother may not be watching us; but we are all watching Big Brother.

Tolstoy tried to explode the Great Man view of history. He substitutes for it a scheme of trends and movements. The wise man is not Napoleon who thinks he controls events, but Kutuzov, who knows he does not, but allows himself to be midwife to a natural process. Yet when Tolstoy comes to trends and movements, he falters, because he knows a movement is like the canals on Mars — an optical illusion which scatters into discrete particles, at a higher resolving power. That is why his immense Epilogue is self-contradictory. Any *scheme* of history is self-contradictory, because it is in some sense a metaphor. To quote a contemporary, 'Life is like nothing, because it is everything.'[1]

Of course, Tolstoy only examines war as a convenient way of examining the nature of society. A general's ignorance and helplessness were matched in the nineteenth century by the helplessness of the ruler and the liberal. They had neither information nor control. They worked in the fog of peace. If I may stick my neck out still farther into someone else's business, I would suggest that we have here the solution to an old question. Amid the common sense and good indignation of nineteenth-century Marxism, there stands, like a monument to the frailty of reason, the image of a future which never came to pass.

[1] *Free Fall*, by William Golding.

The revolution was to start among highly industrialized peoples. But Marx lacked the sort of imagination which you find in the best science fiction. He could not foresee that what was to suffer the most important dialectical change of all was the nature of communication. It is precisely because in a highly industrialized society the sheer volume of the means of communication produces a new quality, that revolutions do not happen there. The effect of the ease, the immediacy and complexity of communications is to make the control of such a nation as certain as the control of a familial group once was. Communism rose in backward, illiterate, centrifugal Russia and China. You can only communize a highly industrialized country in the presence, and with the backing, of an exterior, overwhelming force. Those people who said casually that the BBC saved the country from revolution during the General Strike were nearer the mark than those who awarded the palm to British amiability. The workers got a Reith's-eye view of Old England.

Instruments and victims of the uncontrolled Napoleonic war were those hundred or so characters who inhabit the fringe of Tolstoy's book. Any half-dozen of them would make a Jane Austen novel. They are drawn with just such an exquisite and ironic pen. Old Count Rostov, incapable of doing anything but give parties, as a queen bee is incapable of doing anything but lay eggs; Prince Vassili, lazy, selfish and methodical; Ellen, his cold, sensual daughter; Anna Pavlovna; Alpatich — they come storming into the mind, with armies of bedraggled soldiers and peasants, once attention is directed away from the centre. Over them all loom the figures of Napoleon and Kutuzov, flame-lit and massive as Gog and Magog.

At the centre are those characters whom we know as we know life itself. We can argue about Natasha, as we can argue about Mary, Queen of Scots. That sketched relationship between Prince Bolkonsky and his wife has the awful validity of the people just up the road. At the centre of the centre is bumbling Pierre, ego, *homo præsans*, I, home, this creature, knowledgeable and ignorant, incompetent at bed and duel, tremulous, wealthy, astonished, slave of five appetites, slothful and vigorous, selfish and generous, educated and undedicated, an awareness of living, with nothing to lose but his brains. We know them and we do not understand them, nor did Tolstoy. Is not the greatness of the book measurable by the number of circumstances in which he implicitly admits his own defeat? Men felt exhilaration in battle. They died willingly for a man they did not know, thinking it an honour. Natasha was unfaithful; and the objective description comes across great gaps in causality. Perhaps Tolstoy was saying to life what the face of Princess Bolkonsky said to her husband after she had died in childbirth: 'Why did you do this to me?'

Indeed, the changes in focal length, from set battle piece to domestic interior — the philosophical jaunts, the analyses, the relations between people in all their indefinable complexity: these make it impossible for the reader to do anything but pick his individual path through the woods. After all, *War and Peace* is more than a mountain; it is a world.

Exhaustion supervenes. What is there more to say? One thing is certain. Count Tolstoy's book is not for summer reading. No one will devour it on the orchard wall or sitting idly in the swing. It should be read lying on a Russian stove, with snow piled to the eaves. It is a book to defeat Generals November, December, January, February, March. But it leaves this reader at any rate feeling that he should burn incense before it or set about salaaming — as natives are said to salaam before rock formations which are obscurely meaningful and have on their vast surfaces the print of a more than human thumb.

On the Crest of the Wave

What does the immediate future hold for the novelist in this country? Is there any change in the intellectual climate which can be predicted? What is universal education bringing us? Before making any large statements — which are bound, by the nature of things, to be partial and inaccurate — I had better set out my qualifications and disqualifications for doing so.

I have never taught in a university and I know nothing about publishing; but I have taught English for twenty years in a large grammar school, and I have been trying to write the sort of thing I would define as 'Significant Literature' for longer than that. For fifteen years I travelled the countryside, lecturing in villages and hamlets, taking classes of adults in towns and cities and army camps. I am by nature an optimist; but a defective logic — or a logic which I sometimes hope desperately is defective — makes a pessimist of me.

The fifties and early sixties are a splendid time for bookmen. We may laugh at or deplore the vast circulation of certain periodicals and books; but they do not take the place of anything better. They are an addition. We are on the crest of a wave of universal education, able to look forward to the land and, behind us, out to sea. We are high up, in fact, and the wave has not yet broken, to run on in a neat bank of dwindling foam. We are — and I shall try to show why I think this — the educational millennium. The change started more than a century ago with the Hundred Best Books, a library to bring the worthiest that has been thought and said within reach of the lower orders, at sixpence a time.

I examine the *History of Herodotus*, specially translated for that library. It has slabs of small, grey print, less readable than Rawlinson, less faithful than Bohn. The liveliest, easiest and most entertaining of histories has become a chore, a duty that only a passionate determination to be educated could stay with to the end. Yet I remember hearing of one man who read the whole library, book by book. He was a miner and lay reader. What time he spent on the surface was devoted to the Lord's work. Yet he knew there was another sphere, apart from coal and the Lord, a sphere we might call the humanities, or culture, or education.

The Bible was not enough, neither were Paley, *The Serious Call*, *The Saint's Rest*, the *Concordance*, Wesley's *Journal*, Josephus, or *Grace Abounding*. There was a guessed-at brightness apart from these, and he thirsted for it in a way which must have troubled him because it was worldly by his rigid standards. Finally, after who knows what searching of conscience, he concluded that he had a little leisure every day to spare from coal and God. In the mornings he used a pair of bellows to blow up the fire. He rigged an attachment to the bellows and worked it with his foot. As the fire began to glow in the darkness of a winter's dawn, he would read a paragraph; and because he was a remarkable man, dedicated, he would learn the paragraph by heart. He was an ancestor of mine — if the word is permissible in such an ordinary family — and I know nothing more about him; but the tradition of the bellows has persisted. And we live, as far as this third, worldly activity is concerned, in his millennium.

I remember a picture that is relevant. H. G. Wells describes it somewhere. Two radiantly beautiful children, a boy and a girl, clean children, magnificent specimens both, are looking into the dawn. One of those hygienic and comely women who haunted Wells's imagination is kneeling by them, her arm round their shoulders, and she is pointing into the light. She is Education.

Fervently I agree. Education should be like that, can be like that, *is* sometimes like that. I know those children, have taught them. I think back to the sixth forms of the twenties and contrast them with the sixth forms I teach now. Grammar school boys in the twenties were smaller, half-starved, some of them, often dirty, thin, bitter, lively. They fought swarmingly for a place in the sun. *Their* children are the children of the picture, moving up the escalator until I meet them as sixth formers, large, clean, magnificent physical specimens who could throw me out of the window — men as different from their fathers as Californian fruit is from a crab apple. Yes, the children of the picture are with us already.

But what has happened to the woman? She is still there all right. But she is different. Though she tends to think now in sub-sections, she cannot be called a civil servant precisely, for that would imply a degree of honest direction which is foreign to our native hypocrisy. Therefore she does not wear the Post Mistress's blouse and skirt. She still wears the near-classical robes which symbolize the true, the beautiful and the good. But her face is fretted with the lines of worry and exasperation. The hand across the shoulders holds a pair of scales so that the children can see how this thing in this pan weighs more than the other one. A pair of dividers hangs from her little finger so that they can check that this thing is longer than that. Her right hand still points into the dawn, but the little girl is yawning; and the boy is looking at his feet. For the worry and exasperation in Education's face are because she has learnt something herself: that the supply of teachable material is as limited as the supply of people who can teach; that neither can be manufactured or bought anywhere; and lastly, most important of all — a thought that turns her exasperation into panic — she is pointing the children in one direction and being moved, herself, in another.

We are like the man who pays lip-service to culture and quiet and meditation; but who shows by his actions that the thing he really believes in is making a fortune. He is so surrounded by things, that he tries to have the lot; and ends by doing nothing or tagging along behind the shaming thing that attracts his appetites. Education still points to the glorious dawn, officially at any rate, but has been brought to see, in a down-to-earth manner, that what we really want is technicians and civil servants and soldiers and airmen and that only she can supply them. She still calls what she is doing 'education' because it is a proper, a dignified word — but she should call it 'training', as with dogs. In the Wellsian concept, the phrase she had at the back of her mind was 'Natural Philosophy'; but the overtones were too vast, too remote, too useless on the national scale, too emphatically on the side of 'knowing' rather than 'doing'.

Now I suppose that I had better admit that all this is about 'Science' in quotation marks, and I do so with fear and trembling. For to attack 'Science' is to be labelled reactionary; and to applaud it, the way to an easy popularity. 'Science' has become a band-waggon on which have jumped parsons and television stars, novelists and politicians, every public man, in fact, who wants an easy hand-up, all men who are either incapable of thought or too selfishly careerist to use it; so that the man in the street is persuaded by persistent half-truths that 'Science' is the most important thing in the world, and Education has been half-persuaded, too. But it cannot be said often enough or loudly enough that 'Science' is not the most important thing. Philosophy is more important than 'Science'; so is history; so is courtesy, come to that, so is aesthetic perception. I say nothing of religion, since it is outside the scope of this article; but on the the national scale, we have come to pursue naked, inglorious power when we thought we were going to pursue Natural Philosophy.

The result of this on the emotional climate is perceptible already. Mind, I have no statistical evidence to present; unless convictions that have grown out of experience may be called unconsciously statistical. I recognize that everything I say may be nothing more than an approximation to the truth, because the truth itself is so qualified on every side, so slippery that you have to grab at it as, and how, you can. But we are on the crest of the wave and can see a little way forward.

It is possible when writing a boy's report to admit that he is not perfect. This has always been possible; but today there is a subtle change and the emphasis is different. You can remark on his carelessness; you can note regretfully his tendency to bully anyone smaller. You can even suggest that the occasions when he removed odd coins from coats hung in the changing room are pointers to a deep unhappiness. Was he perhaps neglected round about the change of puberty? Does he not need a different father-figure; should he not therefore, try a change of psychiatrist? You can say all this; because we all live in the faith that there is some machine, some expertise that will make an artificial silk purse out of a sow's ear. But there is one thing you must not say because it will be taken as an irremediable insult to the boy and to his parents. *You must not say he is unintelligent.* Say that and the parents will be after you like a guided missile. They know that intelligence cannot be bought or created. They know, too, it is the way to the good life, the shaming thing, that we pursue without admitting it, the naked power, the prestige, the two cars and the air travel. Education, pointing still, is nevertheless moving their way; to the world where it is better to be envied than ignored, better to be well-paid than happy, better to be successful than good—better to be vile, than vile-esteemed.

I must be careful. But it seems to me that an obvious truth is being neglected. Our humanity, our capacity for living together in a full and fruitful life, does not reside in knowing things for the sake of knowing them or even in the power to exploit our surroundings. At best these are hobbies and toys — adult toys, and I for one would not be without them. Our humanity rests in the capacity to make value judgments, unscientific assessments, the power to decide that this is right, that wrong, this ugly, that beautiful, this just, that unjust. Yet these are precisely the questions which 'Science' is not qualified to answer with its measurement and analysis. They can be answered only by the methods of philosophy and the arts. We are confusing the immense power which the scientific method gives us with the all-important power to make the value judgments which are the purpose of human education.

The pendulum has swung too far. There was a time in education — and I can just remember it — when science fought for its life, bravely and devotedly. Those were the days when any fool who had had Homer beaten into his arse was thought better educated than a bright and inquiring Natural Philosopher. But now the educational world is full of spectral shapes, bowing acknowledgments to religious instruction and literature but keeping an eye on the laboratory where is respect, jam to-morrow, power. The arts are becoming the poor relations. For the arts cannot cure a disease or increase production or ensure defence. They can only cure or ameliorate sicknesses so deeply seated that we begin to think of them in our new wealth as built-in: boredom and satiety, selfishness and fear. The vague picture of the future which our political parties deduce from us as a desirable thing is limitless prosperity, health to enable us to live out a dozen television charters, more of everything; and dutifully they shape our education so that the picture can be painted in.

The side effect is to enlarge the importance of measurement and diminish the capacity to make value judgments. This is not deliberate and will be denied anyway. But when the centre of gravity is shifted away from the social virtues and the general refining and developing of human capacities, because that is not what we genuinely aspire to, no amount of lip-service and face-saving can alter the fact that the change is taking place. Where our treasure is, there are our hearts also.

So, at last, how does this affect the novel as a form demanding something from the reader? It reduces to nothing, to begin with, all but the strongest and most exceptional native taste. The appreciation of the power of expression in all its richness is dimmed. The vitality of writing — that energy of conception and expression which can give passionate significance to an apparent commonplace — this vitality has to fight another layer of imperception. I can describe a way in which this comes about — a way at once ridiculous and subtle. In many schools — in most, for all I know — boys spend a considerable fraction of their time writing up experiments. They are taught to report the phenomena in a detached way. 'One gram of sodium chloride was placed in a test tube and ten cubic centimetres of water were added. . . .' On and on they go, using their own language with the grey precision of an electronic computer, laying it over the world of things, like a dishcloth. Is it any wonder that writers seem to them to use a language they have to learn all over again? They recognize categories of book, as though they were just beginning Greek and judging whether or no the book is written as poetry, by the length of the lines.

For the pressure is too great, the emphasis too obvious. Boys do not evaluate a book. They divide books into categories. There are sexy books, war books, westerns, travel books, science fiction. A boy will accept anything from a section he knows rather than risk another sort. He has to have a label on the bottle and know it is the mixture as before. You must put his detective story in a green paperback or he may suffer the hardship of reading a book in which nobody is murdered at all.

I am not thinking now of the genuine scientist, the natural

philosopher. He is, at most, part of one per cent. Such a boy or man is intelligent enough to move outside his own subjects and find what there is for him among the arts. He is likely to discover the novel or poetry while the inferior intellectual material left on the art's side is giving up wrestling with it. I am thinking more of the plodders, the amiable majority of us, not particularly intelligent or gifted; well-disposed, but left high and dry among a mass of undigested facts with their scraps of saleable technology. What chance has literature of competing with the defined categories of entertainment which are laid on for them at every hour of the day? I do not see how literature for them is to be anything but simple, repetitive and a stop-gap for when there are no westerns on the telly. They will have a far less brutish life than their nineteenth-century ancestors, no doubt. They will believe less and fear less. But just as bad money drives out good so inferior culture drives out superior. With any capacity to make value judgments vitiated or undeveloped, what mass future is there, then, for poetry, for belles-lettres, for real fearlessness in the theatre, for the novel which tries to look at life anew, in a word, for intransigence? Writers who aim at selling their work — surely a minimal dignity to hope for — will be forced more and more to conform to stereotyped patterns, to formulas, to giving the public all it can take.

WESTWARD LOOK

A Touch of Insomnia

The unaccustomed susurration of the ventilators reminded me vividly of things I would sooner forget; and in any case, the enormous meals, the day-long indolence, had made great nature's second course unattainable. It was not the Company's fault, bless them. They tried, with the boundless but unimaginative good will of all nannies, to give their charges a routine which was what those charges wanted, and at the same time did them good. Nanny knew (for she had been ashore once, when there was no servant problem and nice people had begun to accept the horseless carriage), Nanny knew that God had ordained the precise structure of Edwardian England, and that any change would be for the worse. She petted us. She prepared us for, then kept us in, that station to which the Company had called us. Moaning beneath the ventilator, I cursed the exactness of the social image which she called a ship.

Here the class system was axiomatic. You could not invade a plusher bar simply by readiness to pay more. Nor could you descend to a comfortable pub if you wanted to pay less. Where you were born, there you stayed. At the beginning — a sort of privileged babyhood — you could glimpse the other worlds. You could pass through doors marked First Class and see the wide bedrooms, the stupendous still lifes of sea food on the side tables of the dining-room. Perhaps this was a concession to our brief stop in republican France — for after that, the doors were locked. We had to be content with our middle station, right aft, where you got any vibration that was going. And I supposed there was some sealed-off hold where the base of our social pyramid rested; where tourists were chained to the kelson under the whips of savage taskmasters, while their flesh was subdued by a diet of weevily biscuit and stale water.

Nevertheless, I had to admit this was a Brave New World; for why should anyone repine at the more luxurious fate of another, or take thought for the unfortunate, when he was lulled by soft-foot service, by preposterous food and glitter into acquiescence? Turning restlessly beneath the ventilator, I fingered my belly again and understood why a photograph of an Edwardian shooting party is little more than a display of stomachs. Here, there were five courses for breakfast, with a coaxing steward who seemed genuinely disappointed if the master preferred only one; six courses for lunch; seven for dinner; in between times, cups of tea, bowls of nourishing soup; and all tendered with the gentle implication that you were convalescent after a long illness and should build yourself up. Then there was the bar — if you were inured to the bumble of a screw — where you could sit and subject the wake to an empty-headed examination.

Was it . . . not the sickness, but the sadness, the *weltschmerz* resulting from the constant movement of the ship which made me so drearily aware of our company? We were, as far as I could discover, the professional classes. We were doctors, lawyers, junior diplomats, supporting actors, scholars, writers not of best-sellers but of books with *réclame*. We were scientists — but not physicists, who by the logic of history, travel First. We had a fair share of American widows who had taken the trip because Elmer always wanted to go; and these were insultingly eager to get back to the States. We had many old people and few children. We could afford to fly, but either feared to or did not care to. Our drinking habits were abstemious, and if we had wine with our meals we generally ordered the half-bottle. Though full of good will, we did not make friends easily. We patronized neither the swimming pool nor the gymnasium, though we talked of doing both. Sometimes we went to the cinema, but with the avowed intention of passing the time. We knew we were not going to enjoy what we saw very much. We wore a darker lounge suit for dinner and found getting out of a deck-chair just that little bit difficult.

Dear Nanny — I thought, as I belched indelicately — should we ever escape from your lavender'd apron? There was Gala Night, for example, a festival for the whole ship. Perhaps deep in her bowels the tourists suddenly found their chains struck off, were given a double helping of pea-soup, a tot of rum and free-dom till the clock tolled twelve. Down there, we had thought — with the nearest we permit ourselves to bitterness — down there, they were probably drinking Guinness and dancing Knees Up, Mother Brown, or doing The Lambeth Walk. Up there, on the other hand, and 200 yards nearer the bows, were lucullan orgies and neronian debauch. Film stars and directors, tycoons and Ministers of the Crown were vying with each other in gross expense. What gods and maidens loth? What pipes and tim-brels? What wild ecstasy?

In our precise enclave we were hardly party-minded, for our migrant scholars were not wandering ones. Yet Nanny did her best. All her charges should have a party, like it or not. At the second sitting for dinner, each person was provided with a small paper hat. We wore miniature shakos, dunces' caps, bonnets and top-hats, while our eyes avoided all human contact and a confused, British silence deepened, broken only by the steady champing of 400 sets of false teeth.

Really, it was too much! I sat up testily, felt for my watch and then I understood.

Going from east to west across the Atlantic, you catch up an hour a day on the sun. The day is twenty-five hours long, a fearsome consideration to me who already find days quite long enough. But this midnight that had come upon us was a hiatus, a suffocating interlude when the clocks stopped and stayed so for an hour. I scrambled out of my bunk, dressed and made my way up to the promenade deck, through a blaze of deserted lights. What lights they were, with their interminable multiplication in veneer and mirror! Austin Reed's, the Library, the Main Lounge had everything but people. In the bar, when the ship felt a swell, a hundred cases of liquor clashed and rattled. This was The Strand Palace Hotel dumped on Brighton Pier and the whole cut adrift. Because there was no one about, the air was heavy with a sense of Grimm or Poe or SF.

'*Don't you understand, Swithin? Formula X was too successful. We are the only men left alive in the universe!*'

Was I the Flying Dutchman, condemned to sail for ever without landfall? All the clocks, standing grimly to attention at midnight, had stopped time in its stride. Only one other thing moved. Astern, outlined against our stationary wake, a catwalk stretched from one side of the ship to the other; and here, a robot paced, its seaman's hat sliding along the upper edge of the canvas windbreaker as it moved from side to side and paused occasionally to inspect the sheer walls stretching 300 yards ahead of it. It saw my lonely figure and stopped. It watched me closely. Had I perhaps lost my all at Bingo? Had my brain been turned by an hour's talk with three aged widows? To reassure it, I tottered windy and splay-legged under cover again. I remembered those midnight liners one sees from the deck of a small boat. They draw their effulgent length across the night and seem so crowded, such a funfair, a town; but I knew now they were deserted automata with the minimum machine-minders about; and a robot pacing the catwalk astern lest one of the thousand sleepers should decide to end it all.

Still twelve o'clock. In the main lounge the headless chairs discoursed together. It would always be twelve o'clock and we were getting nowhere. We were going very fast on the tread-mill, we were sitting immovably in the exact middle of that tilting, weltering, slopped seaplate which is all the sailor can ever know of the Atlantic Ocean or any other ocean. Up there, in the heights of our society at the captain's table, they might hope for reassurance, and see their pilot face to face; and down there, in the hold, they could not care less; but here, here in half-way house with its marshal for suicides ——

I was sweating absurdly when every clock in the ship gave a hiccup. Time started again. Already, it was thirty seconds past twelve. We were getting somewhere, of course we were. Was it my fancy that the figure on the catwalk relaxed at that moment, as if knowing we had passed some indefinable crisis, some danger? Twenty-eight knots, westward ho, and all was well. The Master-at-Arms emerged from some cave, on his rounds. He walked busily, but stopped to greet me.

'Not able to sleep, sir?'

There was a shade of rebuke in the greeting, the implication that if Nanny could not rock you to sleep, your case was grave indeed. Firmly determined to be myself, in spite of Nanny, I returned to the promenade deck and started to stump up and down. Faster and faster I went along a hundred yards of careful caulking, from the open door at the afterdeck to the public-address system in the waist. Up and down I went — doing, after all, what Nanny would approve of — chasing, catching, out-distancing that ghastly procession of good meals, in puritanical fervour to crucify my belly — almost as though, since I was taking exercise, I might expect to hear from the public-address system my captain's loud 'Well done'. The clocks speeded up with me. Before I had noticed the trickles of sweat in the crooks of my knees, it was three o'clock. If I were not so learned a navigator, my trigonometry so spherical, I could have per-suaded myself that the greyness over the wake was indeed the dawn. I was sleepy at last. Of *course* we were getting somewhere — onward, ever onward to some morrow which would be another today and so forth. In my bunk, the ventilators sounded positively soothing.

The Glass Door

I don't know how far the Alleghenies stretch. They are the small patch of brown, half-way up the map of America on the right-hand side. They consist of parallel ranges, and cover, I suppose, more area than the British Isles. They are not very distinguished as mountains go. They are relatively low, and tree-clad. They have no violence, but abundant charm. How should they not? They pass through Virginia, where charm is laid on so thick you could saw it off in chunks and export it.

Here, in Virginia, is none of the restless energy, the determined modernity, the revolutionary fervour, which in retrospect I see to have characterized my own country. I crossed the Atlantic from the passionate antagonisms of Salisbury traffic on a market day, to the controlled silence of New York in a rush hour. New York traffic flows in a tide too full for sound or foam, and is peaceful by comparison. I thought then that the allegedly horrifying pace of American life was a European invention; and when I got to Virginia I was certain of it. Shout at Virginia, shake it, slap its face, jump on it — Virginia will open one eye, smile vaguely, and go to sleep again.

Our base of operations is Hollins, a rich girls' college, lapped about by fields, and set down in a fold of the Alleghenies. It is ineffably peaceful. Wherever you look, there are hills looped along the skyline. Every circumstance pleases, woos, soothes, and makes comprehension difficult. We arrived during the Indian summer, when every blade of grass, every leaf, was loaded down with cicadas, each of which seemed to be operating a small dentist's drill. Eagles and buzzards floated a thousand feet up in the hot air. Blue jays played in the fields and a delicately built mocking-bird balanced on the white fence by our window like a lady with a parasol on a tightrope. On the day of our arrival, a mountain bear — probably walking in his sleep —

wandered into the nearby town, saw himself in the glass door of the library, panicked, woke up the neighbourhood, was anaesthetized and taken home again.

Hollins sits among its mountains and fields, remembering the eighteenth century. There is a sulphur spring in the grounds, surrounded by a sort of bandstand. In the old days, mammas would take pallid or spotty daughters here to have them cleared up; and the place became a spa. Judging by the pictures of strolling ladies and young bloods driving curricles, it must have been a thriving marriage market — an activity which it has never wholly lost. But in the 1840s the mammas left, social rooms and dormitories were built, and the place became a college.

Hollins, set in its estate of several hundred acres, grew to be an enclave of colonial architecture, all white pillars and porches, grouped round a quadrangle of grass and splendid trees. Lately, a most expensive chapel has taken the place of the old one. A magnificent library building has been added, modern to the last air-conditioned, glass-fronted detail, where the bookstacks have a most generous expanse of working space round them. It is typical of the almost parody southernism of the place that the laboratories are still inadequate. But I have to admit that this choice of what things come first seems splendidly liberal to me, who have suffered from the contrary conception.

Here, then, we work gently, with cushions under us, and plate glass between us and the rest of the world. It is pleasant to contemplate the clock on the administration buildings, by which we regulate our affairs. For the clock is a Virginian clock. The minute hand toils up, lifting the heavy weight of the hour until it totters upright. Then, as if that effort had exhausted the mechanism, the hand falls down to half past three and stays there, collapsed. Long may it continue so to make a mock of the arbitrary, enslaving time-stream! It is as useless and decorative as the carillon which tinkles out Mozart minuets, or hymns, or snatches of old song, from the chapel spire.

Under the trees, along the cemented paths, go the drifts of girls, sympathetic and charming, giggling or absorbed, shy of the bearded foreigner behind his plate glass, but courteous to the helplessness of old age. Some of them are northerners, but the most part southern, and some are from the deep South. Like all women students, they are inveterate, comically obsessive note-takers, who hope by this method to avoid the sheer agony of having to think for themselves. Often they have an earnestness before the shrine of this unknown god Education, which seems at odds with their careful make-up and predatory scent. They will propose a scheme of studies which leaves them no time to eat in the middle of the day; but 40 per cent of them leave to get married before they reach the end of their studies. They are intimidating, ingenuous, and delightful; and about the realities of life in the world at large they know absolutely nothing at all.

Yet how should they? Problems are smoothed over, and have the sharp edges blunted for them by space, prosperity, and the American capacity for presenting any situation in a series of ready-made phrases. Even that problem in the South, which has made such a stir in the world, does not occur here so acutely, since the coloured population in this neighbourhood is only about 10 per cent of the whole. Certainly it exists; and an Englishman, who sees everything at one remove, understands not only the discourtesy of meddling with it, but the difficulty of dealing with the problem precisely because it is *not* acute. Hollins is an enclave, an educated and liberal one. It has preserved almost as an archaeological relic what was inoffensive in the white/black pattern, without perhaps noticing what was going on.

Across the field outside our window is a wood, under Tinker Mountain. In the wood, and partly visible, is a hamlet, a red church with a white, clapboard spire. This is a Negro village. In the old days, when girls came to Hollins, they brought their body slaves with them, and sometimes these slaves stayed on. They settled in the hamlet, and now provide the servants for the college. I see them every afternoon, making their dignified way across the field, large, comfortable women in bright clothes, young men who go whistling and with a dancing step. As your eyes grow accustomed to the light of this ancient country, you begin to see that the man who empties your ashcan is coloured; so are the men who sweep your road or work in the power-house, so are the girls who clean or wash or sew, or serve in the canteen. Yet at Hollins, because of its isolation, the relationship is a historical relic. What keeps a girl out of Hollins is not a colour bar but an economic one. It costs more than $2,800 a year to keep a girl there.

For the problem is smoothed over, is down out of sight. The servants, like college servants everywhere, have a long tradition of service. They seem proud of the college and the college is proud of them. Here, embalmed, is a tiny section, a left-over bit of history, which loyalty, education and kindliness have minimized until it has a sort of willow-pattern charm. Yet north of us is an area where the public schools have shut down to avoid integration. South of us, the railway has segregated waiting rooms.

The problem is at once too foreign, too vast, and too muted for my comprehension. At least there is a fund of human goodwill here, which makes the cheap jibes flung from outside seem blunted weapons. Let me do no more, therefore, than record a scene, before the adjustments, the manoeuvres, the shrugs of history have taken it away for ever. I emerged the other day from a book-lined room to the shock of autumn's air on the campus. A dozen coloured men stood by leaf-piles, with brooms and rakes in their hands. Some of them talked, and pushed the leaves about. Others stood motionless, leaning on rakes. They wore bright blue and red, rich brown. They worked, when they worked, with inspired slowness, under the Virginian clock. Silhouetted against the white columns, among thick trunks and clattering leaves, standing among drifts of girls who tinkled here and there with laughter, the dark men seemed a still life. They seemed happy to do this, as the girls seemed happy to do that. Passing among them in the brisker air, some obscure compulsion made me speak to the oldest man of all. He was small and gnarled, dressed in bright blue, his black face startling under a stubble of white hair. I made some inane remark about the weather, which woke him up. He laughed and crowed, and his body jerked. 'Yas-suh!' he said; and we both knew, with one of those psychic flashes that are so often wrong, that we were taking part in some ripe old comedy of the South — 'Yas-suh!'

I reeled on, conscious at last of my solid presence in this mild, foreign land, and struck myself a shattering blow on the invisible glass door of the library. I tottered inside as the carillon tinkled out a minuet by Mozart; and sank into a seat among the girls who were studying the mythological sources of Oedipus and Hamlet, or surveying Spanish Literature, or reading *The Rights of Man*.

For the problem has not yet come consciously to Hollins. Perhaps it never will, but be by-passed. Yet the enclave is not secure. As the town expands, the value of the Hollins land goes up and presently there will be pressure to sell. Moreover, now that America has inherited an ancient mantle, exotic students are coming to Hollins; Indian and Korean, like the business interests pressing south into Virginia, they are a sign of things to come. They are a colourful sight, in the national costume which is their only defence against the ancient intolerance of the countryside. Moreover, an inter-State highway is advancing across the land, majestically shouldering hills out of its way; and like it or not, that road will divide the estate not half a mile from the campus.

Yet for today, preserved, there stands the pattern; the friendly faculty, the girls, the tall, colonial columns, the dark servants and the quiet sun.

Body and Soul

East Coast blanked out from North Carolina right up to the Canadian border; a half-continent under a pat of fog; nothing visible but the extreme tip of the Empire State Building; planes grounded. Fog, the airman's common cold; all the resources of science are squeaking and gibbering under it; lights blink unseen, radar echoes quiver and ping; the gigantic aircraft lumber round the ramps and aprons like death's-head moths in cold weather; money leaks away. We, the privileged, sit in a sort of underground air-raid shelter, racked by public-address systems and blasts of furious air-conditioning. Evening drags into night. Everything is astonishingly dirty, and time itself is stale. We sit.

Most passengers drift away, to go by train, or try a night's sleep in the airport hotel. But I am going too far to get there any way but by jet. Tomorrow I give the first of three lectures in Los Angeles, on the other side of America. Here it is midnight, or past midnight, or feels like midnight. I am late already, and must go by what flight I can. I cannot telegraph anyone, even though I shall land at the wrong airport.

A loudspeaker honks and burbles. Incredibly, and for the next hour, we have take-off and landing limits. Our plane is getting through; and sure enough, presently it bumbles out of the fog from the runway. I go with our group to Gate Nine, shudder into a freezing night with a dull grey roof. The jet crawls towards us, howling and whistling with rage, perhaps at the fog or perhaps at the human bondage which keeps it only just under control. For a moment or two, it faces us — no, is end-on to us; for here there is no touch of human, or animal, or insect, no face — only four holes that scream like nothing else in creation. Then it huddles round and is still. Doors open and two streams of passengers ooze out. Their faces are haggard. They ignore the

145

night that has caught up with them. They stagger, or walk with the stiff gait of stage sleep-walkers. One or two look stunned, as if they know it is midnight more or less but cannot remember if it is today or tomorrow midnight and why or what. Strange vehicles flashing all over with red lights come out of the darkness, not for the passengers, but to tend the jet. They crouch under the wings and the front end, attach themselves by tubes while all their lights flash, and lights on the jet flash, and the engines sink from a wail to a moan — a note, one might think, of resignation, as if the machine now recognizes that it is caught and will have to do the whole thing over again. But for half an hour they feed it well, while it sucks or they blow, and we stand, imprisoned by the freezing cold and our own need to be somewhere else. Jet travel is a great convenience.

Then we are in, fastening safety belts, and I peer out of the window with a naïveté which seems to increase as I grow older; and a succession of blue lights flick by faster and faster; and there is an eternity of acceleration at an angle of forty-five degrees, while the whistling holes under the wings seem no longer angry but godlike — see what we can do! Look, no hands! The 'No Smoking, Fasten Your Safety Belts' notice disappears. Cupping my hands round my face, squinting sideways and down, I can make out that there is a white pat of fog slipping by beneath us, and over it a few stationary stars. An air hostess demonstrates the use of the oxygen masks.

Comfort, warmth flowing back into rigid hands, comparative silence, stillness except for an occasional nudge as the plane pierces a furlong of turbulence; I try to think of what our airspeed means: it remains nothing but arithmetic. The interior of the plane is like a very superior bus. Am thawed and relaxed. They say that this is not the latest mark of jet — do jets come any faster or bigger or plusher?

Glasses tinkle. Air Hostess brings round drinks — not what happens in a bus. Select Bourbon. (Always live off the country as far as possible.) I also secrete the TWA swizzlestick as a memento. Do not cross America often this way. Another Bourbon. That makes the two obligatory drinks before an American dinner. Am cheerful now — but second drink did not contain swizzlestick and wonder if I am detected? Air Hostess approaches for the third time and I cower — but no. She is

146

English and recognizes a fellow-countryman. Speaks Kensingtonian, which sounds odd at this place and altitude. (Note to intending immigrants. Kensingtonian despised in a man. Gets him called a pouf. Do not know exactly what this terms means, but cannot think it complimentary. On the other hand, Kensingtonian in a girl widely approved of, Americans think it cute.)

Peripeteia! English Air Hostess has read my books and seen me on English telly! I instantly acquire overwhelming status. Feel utterly happy and distinguished in a nice, diffident, English sort of way. Neighbour puts away his briefcase — we all have briefcases — then talks to me. Is physicist, naturally. Tells me about jets sucking air in at one end and blowing result of combustion out at the other. Encourage him, from a pure sense of *joie de vivre*. Rash, this, very. Tells me about navigation lights, navigation, fluids, including the sea, acceleration — Bourbon now dying down. Make my way forward to lavatory in diffident but distinguished manner, watched by all the unhappy briefcases who haven't been on telly, or haven't been noticed there by an Air Hostess. Lavatory wonderful, buttons everywhere. Push the lot, just to tell grandchildren. Tiny, ultimate fraction of our airstream is scooped in somewhere and directed to blow a jet vertically up out of the pan. Could balance celluloid balls on it and shoot them down with a rifle, as at fairs.

Return to seat and physicist continues course. American Air Hostess comes and talks. More status. Physicist goes to sleep. English Air Hostess comes and talks about London, Paris, Rome, Athens. American Air Hostess counters with Hawaii and Japan. Slight loss of status. I would like to go to sleep. Body here, can see it sitting in the seat. Soul still leaving Atlantic coast. Time? AHs have got on to books. It's the beard, I think. Beard down there on the deck, just beard. Beard in jet v. distinguished. Bourbon quite dead. Return to lavatory for a bit of peace in less distinguished manner. Jet still playing and cannot be bothered to push all the buttons. Return. Physicist says 'Di!' very loudly in his sleep. Die? Diana? Diathermy? AHs wander away. Nod. Have instant vision of Ann with sweeper on carpet. She switches it off, switches off all the sweepers in the world, they fade, whining — am started awake — oh my God, my God! 'No Smoking, Fasten Your Safety Belts' — briefcases stirring like sea-life under returning tide.

Am awake, dammit, or rather body is awake; soul two thousand miles behind, passing through Nashville, Tennessee, shall never be whole again, body mouldering in the jet, soul marching on towards Denver. Time? Bump, rumble, rumble, lights, lights! Los Angeles. Time? Enter Belshazzar's Hall. Body finds hall moving slowly, but they can't fool body. Body knows the movement is the world turning to catch up. More halls, enough for whole dynasties of Belshazzars.

Soul will enjoy this when it catches up. More halls, *Mene, mene.* Briefcases have vanished. Tunnels, fountains, lights, music, palms, lights, more halls — they would have to put *Mene, mene* out by roneograph, or use the public-address system. *A message for Mr. Belshazzar!* Am delirious, I think. Find broom supporting man in centre of hundredth hall. Body asks broom politely. 'Which way is out, Bud?' Broom answers politely, 'Don't arst me, Bud, we just built it.' More halls. Movement of earth deposits body in cab which hurls it ten thousand miles through lights to a recommended English-type hotel. Body recognizes bed as English. Has knobs at each corner. Body falls on bed, giggling at thought of soul now plodding through Death Valley. Body undresses so as to get an hour or two of sleep, telephone rings. Bearleader would like to show body the sights. Body dresses and descends. Nice bearleader drives body through sunny Los Angeles and up the heights where the fire was. Body sees mountain road of burnt houses for film stars. Only thing left is row of swimming pools built on stilts out over the gorge, since there is nowhere else for them.

Descent to Pacific. Waves coming the wrong way — no, that was the Atlantic. Sherry in house. Lunch in university. Forty thousand students, or is it seventy? Own campus police and bus service. After lunch, body looks at lecture notes, but cannot bring itself to care. Body gives first lecture and hears its mouth making the appropriate noises. Soul not really necessary in this game. Has drinks beneath original Beerbohm cartoons. Has dinner with the Christmas Story lining the road outside, each tableau the size of a cottage with full-size figures in plaster and floodlit. Party after dinner. Body is told about the definitive Dickens and the Boswell factory. Body is nearly frightened to hear itself advise against the export of American novels. Stick to cars, it says. Soul would be very angry if it could hear that. Body finds itself getting smaller, or is it larger? Is led away, and falls on English-type bed with knobs at each corner.

At two o'clock in the morning there seemed to be a second person present. With the sort of effort one makes to achieve binocular vision, they united themselves; and soul in body, I was looking at the ceiling of a hotel bedroom in Los Angeles. The luxury of being whole was such that I could not sleep, but smoked till I felt like stockfish. The real trouble was that I had a defect of imagination which would not let me believe I was where I was, and yet I knew I was in Los Angeles. Being whole, I was immediately frightened at the vision of tomorrow's lecture and began to compose it in my sleepless head. That way the day dawned, and just as I ran out of cigarettes, my nice bearleader telephoned to set up the morning's sightseeing. We saw the Mormon temple, with a gold angel on the tower, far larger than any God has in heaven. We saw the colossal Medical Centre where the corridors run clean out of perspective to infinity at a point; where the patient is taken in at one end and can be served up as a complete set of demonstration slides at the other. We saw the beach — and for a moment I was really where I was — watching the waves turn over, and stunned by the acute realization that this had been here all the time, had not been created in Europe and exported to form part of a set. I lectured again, pleaded for an evening in bed, but sneaked off on my own — *peccavi* — and had dinner; filet mignon and a bottle of burgundy-type wine. (Note for wines-men: it was an Almaden '57; suffered like all California wines from that fatal inferiority complex — but once convinced you were a friend, it would offer you what it had.) At two in the morning carried my filet mignon and my burgundy-type wine back to my English-type bed, and lay with my head full of tomorrow's lecture. Dawn.

Nice bearleader came and took me to see the San Gabriel mountains with snow on them and the Chinese Theatre, its pavements with footprints, handprints, graffiti of film stars on them; showed me Hollywood, Gangster's Corner, Mae West's hotel, the William Andrews Clarke Memorial Library. For ten ridiculously exciting seconds I held the MS of *The Importance of Being Earnest* in my hands. (You, too, have been awarded an Oscar!) We finished that jaunt in a bowling alley, where the beer was good, the telly in colour and the machines for setting up the pins seemed, in their implacable devotion, to be much more intelligent than anything else in sight.

I lecture, meet students, and pack grip in a flash. Meet faculty. Party. Nth, I think. Now I am taken to dinner in an English-type restaurant to make me feel at home. Recognize it as English instantly, because the bartender and all the waiters are in full hunting kit. At one moment they gather round a table and sing 'Happy Birthday' in close harmony. Los Angeles is the mostest, am utterly happy. What other place et cetera. Am eating abalone, the local must, and talking in six directions at once, but am suddenly seized and rushed away to jet, leaving soul still continuing conversations. Body loses way down to plane and is nearly sucked through engine, ha ha. Acceleration and fifty miles *square* of lights tilts under us. This is the latest mark of jet, they say, can see no difference, that is the Pacific down there, time, eleven o'clock.

American Air Hostess brings round Bourbon. Secrete swizzlestick. Another Bourbon. American Southern Belle-type Air Hostess, v. pretty, guesses I am English and a writer (beard in jet), comes and sits! Immense status SBAH did Creative Writing Course at College. Said to her Prof. : 'Ah aim to be a writer.' Prof. said : 'What do you know about life?' SBAH said : 'Ah hev written a critical essay on Thomas Wolfe and a short story which ah would like you to read.' Prof. read story, said : 'Go and be an Air Hostess' — 'So heah ah em!' Delightful girl, there ought to be a lot more of them and there probably are. Supper. Go to lavatory and discover this really *is* the latest mark of jet. Tiny, ultimate fraction of our airstream is scooped in somewhere, led into the pan and merely chases itself round and round and round.

Am tucked up solicitously for the night, but am still able to see out of the window, my goodness me, no sleep with a view like that. America sliding by, 650 miles an hour airspeed with 150 miles an hour tail wind; 800 miles an hour over the ground — no cloud. Cities, gleaming, glowing ravishments slide under us six miles down, lines of phosphorescence scored at right-angles to each other. Moon and snow. Stars, perceptibly wheeling. More molten cities. Body understands that America is crust of earth with fire inside, must break out somewhere, hence these scores, these right-angled lava cracks, these chessboard patterns of luminosity (with here and there a wink of veritable incandescence like the white spark on a red coal), but all soft as the tiny lights of a shock cradle. Garish street lamps, Christmas Decorations, traffic signals, window displays, sky signs, now softened, softened. Body lines up jet-hole with city — sees it swallow a whole street six miles long in seconds, how to take the children to school, scoop! three blocks of run-down houses, park, Motel, Motel, Motel, parking lot, cemetery, jump the sparking traffic lights, scoop! Drugstore, Charlies Cheeseburgers, Eats, Frolic Fashion House, Beautician, Physician, Mortician, Realty, News Office WinnDixie MountjoyToy-TownSurplusWarStockCrossroadsChurchofChrist(Airconditioning.)Square!MayoraltyFireStationPoliceStationHoward JohnsonSquare!LightsLightsLightsSquare!LightsLightsLights RiverSquare! All sucked in and blown out, scooped up, hurled back, august, imperial, god-like, America, oh from up here and at this power, even unto weeping, America The ——

SBAH is tinkling glasses and switching on lights. My God. BREAKFAST! Four hours out from Los Angeles — where soul is still engaged in fierce discussion of freedom, birth control, how to be happy though British, Emblems — four hours out, there is ahead of us the distinction between grey and black that betokens dawn over the curved Atlantic. Sure enough, the sweeper is switched off for a thirty-minutes' descent. Poor soul, no longer the centre of my sinful earth, but setting out just now on that long climb over the Rockies. Fasten your safety belts. And the time is. . . .

Gradus ad Parnassum

It is perhaps fortunate, as well as understandable, that I have never held a position of authority in the educational world. Faced with an experiment or a new process in teaching I find myself wholly unable to make up my mind about it. During this last academic year in America I made my first acquaintance with Creative Writing, and still don't know what to think. As you revolve from campus to campus, it will be surprising if you do not find yourself booked to attend a Creative Writing class. It can be a frightening experience; for the visiting novelist finds himself among a group of people who seem to know more about the job than he does. Not only the presiding professor but all the students have a far closer grip on analysis, and a full professional vocabulary for the conduct of a post-mortem. From the mass-production lines of the state universities (50,000 students, perhaps) to the quasi-Oxonian gothic of Yale, the poems, short stories, plays, novels, come pouring out and are put through the critical machine. Nor should they be regarded entirely as juvenilia. Tough publishers take them and sometimes publish them. There are dozens of poetry magazines where the verse may find a home. From my standpoint as a campus visitor, it seemed as though the literary world was being geared more and more directly to the academic one. Among the many authors of standing whom I met in the States, I cannot recollect a single one who had not either been produced by these classes, or some time directed them, or both. This must surely intensify the gap between what is read on campus, and the few books sold in the public drugstore at the other end of the street. In place of mass sales, one of the rewards open to the author is a university position — Writer in Residence — which gives him leisure, adequate pay, and prestige. But it also gets him in the net. Robert Penn Warren at Yale, Eudora Welty at Smith, William

Faulkner at Virginia—whether they needed the money or not, the position ensures that the academic world nibbles at them even if it does not absorb them; and in the States, the academic world, generous, international, complex, is very hard to resist.

The work produced in these seminars tends to fantasy, since it is guaranteed an educated and highly critical audience. It is produced slowly too. Three short stories is a good year's work. Only at Yale did I find something a little more down to earth; a class in which each member had to write so many words each day, just as a pianist does his scales. This means that the average class will contain a few students who have no business to be there at all; but they at least provide an audience for the dedicated writers and at the same time get themselves a credit towards a BA. There is another section, bearded and jeaned, which has ambition and no talent: but in the seminar they can discover this very early. The rest tend to have a spark of talent which is no more than a part of general intelligence. They would be fairly good at anything. Here and there occurs the genuine, bumbling, fettered, uncertain, groping writer, whose work may have none of the smoothness and finish of the student who is content to get by. These, potential authors I suppose, are helped. At least they seem to think so.

The actual classes can be entertaining, boring, moving, funny. At least once, a class achieved the level of embarrassing farce. Let me get the bile out of my system by describing this occasion, far from Virginia, which caused me such pain.

There are, shall we say, seven young men, three girls, a professor, and the peripatetic lecturer. The seven young men and the professor have identical crewcuts. One of the girls is homely and solemn — follows every word with the painstaking care of someone learning a language from discs. One girl is dark, and eager. The third is very pretty and says nothing at all because she does not have to. A choleric crewcut is reading his story in a harsh monotone. As the story goes on the lecturer finds his ears not so much burning as singing, with a high, nightmare note. He does not know where to look. He broods to himself. *I am not tough enough for this game.*

The monotone breaks off and the silence prolongs itself. The lecturer fancies he sees a faint afterglow in the air from the incredible last sentence of the incredible story.

Someone clears his throat.

'Jake, I didn't quite get the symbolism of the hair on the bathmat.'

'It's a sex image.'

More silence. From where he sits, the lecturer can see that the homely girl has written and underscored 'Sex image' in her notes.

'The cookie,' says the eager girl. 'I liked the cookie. I thought it was vivid. There was something about it kinda innocent.'

'It's a sex image.'

The homely girl does some more underscoring. Through the window the lecturer can see a lovely landscape, with a bathing pool and flowers. Suddenly his heart contracts and his eyes seem to come back in like a snail's. The flowers are not for him to pick. After all, this is what he is being paid for. He fumbles through his stock of newly acquired but already worn phrases.

'I was happy with your focal length. But isn't there some obscurity timewise?'

The choleric student turns beetroot.

'Guess I write for myself.'

The lecturer suppresses the unworthy thought that in this case it was perhaps illogical for the author to read his story to an audience.

'Another thing. Does it *carry*?'

Silence. Out of the corner of his eye the lecturer sees the homely girl record: 'Does it carry?'

The professor uncrosses his knees and crosses them the other way.

'I was a bit worried with the plumbing, Jake.'

'It's a sex image.'

The lecturer wades in.

'Let's get the picture clear. This girl, this student. She's making up her mind to have an abortion, isn't she? Motivated by her discovery — since she stopped writing her novel and read his instead — that her professor is really a homosexual and she's basically a lesbian? Yes. I see. Only what I don't see is why you had to make her a spastic.'

'I guess it gives us an extra slant on her professor.'

'It does indeed. Well. My own feeling is that your last two paragraphs are rather low tension. Oughtn't you to work them over again? Otherwise the whole story — '

The words stick in the lecturer's throat. The best he can do is to beam winningly at the author and nod. Everyone else nods too.

'Zing,' murmurs the professor. 'Right on the nose.'

More silence. The pretty girl yawns behind her fist.

'Well,' says the professor briskly. 'Next week. . . .'

Of course there is a sense in which any writer attends creative writing classes. He has to learn the business somehow. What then accounts for my uneasy feeling that to attend these classes is inferior to the hard knocks of making your own way from scratch? Am I a literary rough diamond who insists on his wretched children being just as unhappy as he was? And to *live* with a class, rather than visit one in passing, is another matter; for I never felt my own students, Mark, Anna, Jane, Ben, Betsy, Geneli, could commit anything like these idiocies.

May it be my feeling that we live, not by the work of ten thousand adequate writers, but by the work of a few dozen at most? Creative writing classes are sometimes said to 'take the cork out'. How about the cases where the cork ought to be left in?

— The verses end.

Someone clears his throat.

'Bill. I don't quite get the symbolism of the stars throwing down their spears.'

The professor crosses his knees.

'Well, Harry, I think it's an obvious sex image.'

The homely girl scribbles.

The lecturer clears his throat.

'One small point. Who is "He"?'

'It's the super ego,' says the eager girl. 'I got that. He's controlling the id. He twists the sinews of his heart.'

The homely girl scribbles like mad. The professor is nodding.

'I felt there was some basic confusion in the psychology,' he says. 'You should reread *Totem and Taboo*, Bill. Mind, though, the verses have energy.'

'I'm sticking my neck right out,' says the lecturer, 'but I dare swear we all felt this. Can I have the paper, Bill — it *is* Bill, isn't it? Right. Mmm. You have a positive *cascade* of questions — what hand, what eye, what deeps, skies, wings, what hand, what shoulder, what art, what dread feet, etcetera: and no answers! Not one. Now. Technically, what we have here is the first half of a sonnet. Couldn't you recast it sonnetwise, getting all your questions into the octet? Then in the sestet you could come up with the answers.'

'Zing,' murmurs the professor. 'Right on the nose.'

The lecturer is inspired.

'Why not make it the half of a diptych,' he says. 'Then you could have another set of verses with all the answers to all the questions.'

Everyone nods. The lecturer chants:

> *Framed was my fearful symmetry*
> *By* this *immortal hand and eye. . . .'*

'Where are you going?' cries the professor. 'Hey! Blake! Come back!'

But the author has gone; and borne by some afflatus or other, the pretty girl has disappeared with him.

Yet when all is said and done, these classes are an easy target. And it is worth noting that for better or worse, when Blake leaves them, preferring his own road, he condemns his work to a hundred years of academic indifference. A balanced assessment seems impossible. By posing a paradoxical situation we have raised (like the author) questions with no answers. For the good in the method is obvious too. How can one convey a sense of the thousands, the hundreds of thousands of students who found in these classes a high road to the enjoyment of prose and poetry, a glimpse of the creative process? How can one go against the testimony of dozens of talented professional writers who all claim they were helped, produced even, by creative writing classes?

Well there.

CAUGHT IN A BUSH

Billy the Kid

On the first day, Lily, my nurse, took me to school. We went hand-in-hand through the churchyard, down the Town Hall steps, and along the south side of the High Street. The school was at the bottom of an alley; two rooms, one downstairs and one upstairs, a staircase, a place for hanging coats, and a lavatory. 'Miss' kept the school — handsome, good-tempered Miss, whom I liked so much. Miss used the lower room for prayers and singing and drill and meetings, and the upper one for all the rest. Lily hung my coat up, took me upstairs and deposited me among a score or so of children who ranged in age from five to eleven. The boys were neatly dressed, and the girls over-dressed if anything. Miss taught in the old-fashioned way, catering for all ages at once.

I was difficult.

No one had suggested, before this time, that anything mattered outside myself. I was used to being adored, for I was an attractive child in an Anglo-Saxon sort of way. Indeed, my mother, in her rare moments of lyricism, would declare that I had 'eyes like cornflowers and hair like a field of ripe corn'. I had known no one outside my own family — nothing but walks with Lily or my parents, and long holidays by a Cornish sea. I had read much for my age but saw no point in figures. I had a passion for words in themselves, and collected them like stamps or birds' eggs. I had also a clear picture of what school was to bring me. It was to bring me fights. I lacked opposition, and yearned to be victorious. Achilles, Lancelot and Æneas should have given me a sense of human nobility but they gave me instead a desire to be a successful bruiser.

It did not occur to me that school might have discipline or that numbers might be necessary. While, therefore, I was supposed to be writing out my tables, or even dividing four oranges between two poor boys, I was more likely to be scrawling a list of words, butt (barrel), butter, butt (see goat). While I was supposed to be learning my Collect, I was likely to be chanting inside my head a list of delightful words which I had picked up God knows where — deebriss and Skirmishar, creskant and sweeside. On this first day, when Miss taxed me with my apparent inactivity, I smiled and said nothing, but nothing, until she went away.

At the end of the week she came to see my mother. I stuck my field of ripe corn round the dining-room door and listened to them as they came out of the drawing-room.

My mother was laughing gaily and talking in her front-door voice.

'He's just a little butterfly, you know — just a butterfly!'

Miss replied judiciously.

'We had better let that go for a while.'

So let go it was. I looked at books or pictures, and made up words, dongbulla for a carthorse; drew ships, and aeroplanes with all their strings, and waited for the bell.

I had quickly narrowed my interest in school to the quarter of an hour between eleven and fifteen minutes past. This was Break, when our society at last lived up to my expectations. While Miss sat at her desk and drank tea, we spent the Break playing and fighting in the space between the desks and the door. The noise rose slowly in shrillness and intensity, so that I could soon assess the exact note at which Miss would ring a handbell and send us back to our books. If we were dull and listless, Break might be extended by as much as ten minutes; so there was a constant conflict in my mind — a desire to be rowdy, and a leader in rowdiness, together with the knowledge that success would send us back to our desks. The games were numerous and varied with our sex. The girls played with dolls or at weddings. Most of the time they played Postman's Knock among themselves — played it seriously, like a kind of innocent apprenticeship.

Tap! Tap!
'Who's there?'
'A letter for Mary.'

We boys ignored them with a contempt of inexpressible depth. We did not kiss each other, not we. We played tag or fought in knots and clusters, while Miss drank tea and smiled indulgently and watched our innocent apprenticeship.

Fighting proved to be just as delightful as I had thought. I was chunky and zestful and enjoyed hurting people. I exulted in victory, in the complete subjugation of my adversary, and thought that they should enjoy it too — or at least be glad to suffer for my sake. For this reason, I was puzzled when the supply of opponents diminished. Soon, I had to corner victims before I could get a fight at all.

Imperceptibly the gay picture altered. Once back in our desks, where the boys were safe from me, they laughed at me, and sniggered. I became the tinder to a catch word. Amazed, behind my eager fists, I watched them and saw they were — but what were they? Appearances must lie; for of course they could not drive themselves from behind those aimed eyes, could not persuade themselves that I, ego Billy, whom everyone loved and cherished, as by nature, could not persuade themselves that I was not uniquely woven of precious fabric —

Could it be?

Nonsense! Sky, fly, pie, soup, hoop, croup — georgeous.

But there were whisperings in corners and on the stairs. There were cabals and meetings. There were conversations which ceased when I came near. Suddenly in Break, when I tried to fight, the opposition fled with screams of hysterical laughter, then combined in democratic strength and hurled itself on my back. As for the little girls, they no longer played Postman's Knock, but danced on the skirts of the scrum, and screamed encouragement to the just majority.

That Break ended early. When we were back at our desks, I found my rubber was gone, and no one would lend me another. But I needed a rubber, so I chewed up a piece of paper and used that. Miss detected my fault and cried out in mixed horror and amusement. Now the stigma of dirt was added to the others.

At the end of the morning I was left disconsolate in my desk. The other boys and girls clamoured out purposefully. I wandered after them, puzzled at a changing world. But they had not gone far. They were grouped on the cobbles of the alley, outside the door. The boys stood warily in a semi-circle, their satchels swinging loose like inconvenient shillelaghs. The girls were ranged behind them, ready to send their men into the firing line. The girls were excited and giggling, but the boys were pale and grim.

'Go on!' shouted the girls, 'go on!'

The boys took cautious steps forward.

Now I saw what was to happen — felt shame, and the bitterest of all my seven beings. Humiliation gave me strength. A rolled-up exercise book became an epic sword. I went mad. With what felt like a roar, but must really have been a pigsqueal, I leapt at the nearest boy and hit him squarely on the nose. Then I was round the semi-circle, hewing and thumping like Achilles in the river bed. The screams of the little girls went needle sharp. A second or two later, they and the boys were broken and running up the alley, piling through the narrow entry, erupting into the street.

I stood alone on the cobbles and a wave of passionate sorrow engulfed me. Indignation and affront, shame and frustration took command of my muscles and my lungs. My voice rose in a sustained howl, for all the world as though I had been the loser, and they had chased Achilles back to his tent. I began to zigzag up the alley, head back, my voice serenading a vast sorrow in the sky. My feet found their way along the High Street, and my sorrow went before me like a brass band. Past the Antique Shoppe, the International Stores, Barclay's Bank; past the tobacconist's and the Green Dragon, with head back, and grief as shrill and steady as a siren ——

How can one record and not invent? Is there any point in understanding the nature of a small boy crying? Yet if I am to tell the small, the unimportant truth, it is a fact that my sorrows diminished unexpectedly and woefully up the street. What had been universal, became an army with banners, became soon so small that I could carry it before me, as it were, in two hands. Still indignant, still humiliated, still moving zigzag, with little running impulses and moments of pause, I had my grief where I could hold it out and see it — look! Some complexity of nature added three persons to my seven devils — or perhaps brought three of the seven to my notice. There was Billy grieving, smitten to the heart; there was Billy who felt the unfairness of having to get this grief all the way home where his mother could inspect it; and there was scientific Billy, who was rapidly acquiring know-how.

I suspected that my reservoirs were not sufficient for the waters of lamentation, suspected that my voice would disappear, and that I was incapable of a half-mile's sustained emotion. I began to run, therefore, so that my sorrow would last. When suspicion turned to certainty, I cut my crying to a whimper and settled to the business of getting it home. Past the Aylesbury Arms, across the London Road, through Oxford Street by the Wesleyan Chapel, turn left for the last climb in the Green — and there my feelings inflated like a balloon, so that I did the last twenty yards as tragically as I could have wished, swimming through an ocean of sorrow, all, paradoxically enough, quite, quite genuine — swung on the front door knob, stumbled in, staggered to my mother —

'Why, Billy! Whatever's the matter?'

— balloon burst, floods, tempests, hurricanes, rage and anguish — a monstrous yell —

'THEY DON'T LIKE ME!'

My mother administered consolation and the hesitant suggestion that perhaps some of the transaction had been my fault. But I was beyond the reach of such footling ideas. She comforted, my father and Lily hovered, until at last I was quiet enough to eat. My mother put on her enormous hat and went out with an expression of grim purpose. When she came back, she said she thought everything would be all right. I continued to eat and sniff and hiccup. I brooded righteously on what was going to happen to my school-fellows now that my mother had taken a hand. They were, I thought, probably being sent to bed without anything to eat, and it would serve them right and teach them to like me and not be cruel. After lunch, I enjoyed myself darkly (scaffole, birk, rake), inventing possible punishments for them — lovely punishments.

Miss called later and had a long talk with my mother in the drawing-room. As she left, I stuck my field of ripe corn round the dining-room door again and saw them.

'Bring him along a quarter of an hour late,' said Miss. 'That's all I shall need.'

My mother inclined her stately head.

'I know the children don't really mean any harm — but Billy is so sensitive.'

We were back to normal again, then. That night, I suffered

my usual terrors; but the morning came and I forgot them again in the infinite promise of day. Lily took me to school a quarter of an hour later than usual. We went right in, right upstairs. Everyone was seated and you could have stuck a fork into the air of noiseless excitement. I sat in my desk, Lily went, and school began. Wherever I looked there were faces that smiled shyly at me. I inspected them for signs of damage but no one seemed to have suffered any crippling torment. I reached for a rubber, and a girl in pink and plaits leaned over.

'Borrow mine.'

A boy offered me a handkerchief. Another passed me a note with 'wil you jine my ggang' written on it. I was in. We began to say our tables and I only had to pause for breath before giving an answer to six sevens for a gale of whispers to suggest sums varying from thirty-nine to forty-five. Dear Miss had done her work well, and today I should enjoy hearing her fifteen minutes' homily on brotherly love. Indeed, school seemed likely to come to a full stop from sheer excess of charity; so Miss, smiling remotely, said we would have an extra long break. My heart leapt, because I thought that now we could get on with some really fierce, friendly fighting, with even a bloody nose. But Miss produced a train set. When the other boys got down to fixing rails, the girls, inexpressibly moved by the homily, seized me in posse. I never stood a chance against those excited arms, those tough, silken chests, those bird-whistling mouths, that mass of satin and serge and wool and pigtails and ribbons. Before I knew where I was, I found myself, my cornflowers popping out of my head, playing Postman's Knock.

The first girl to go outside set the pattern.

'A parcel for Billy Golding!'

In and out I went like a weaver's shuttle, pecked, pushed, hugged, mouthed and mauled, in and out from fair to dark to red, from Eunice who had had fever and a crop, to big Martha who could sit on her hair.

I kissed the lot.

This was, I suppose, my first lesson; and I cannot think it was successful. For I did not know about the homily, I merely felt that the boys and girls who tried to do democratic justice on me had been shown to be wrong. I was, and now they knew it, a thoroughly likeable character. I was unique and precious after all; and I still wondered what punishments their parents had found for them which had forced them to realize the truth.

I still refused to do my lessons, confronting Miss with an impenetrable placidity. I still enjoyed fighting if I was given the chance. I still had no suspicion that Billy was anything but perfect. At the end of term, when I went down to Cornwall, I sat in a crowded carriage with my prize book open on my knees for six hours (keroube, serrap, konfeederul), so that passengers could read the inscription. I am reading it now :

BILLY GOLDING
1919
PRIZE FOR
GENERAL IMPROVEMENT

The Ladder and the Tree

For most of my life, childhood, boyhood, and more, we lived at Marlborough. Our house was on the Green, that close-like square, tilted south with the Swindon road running through it. On both sides of the road is grass and the houses that stand round are far older than their Georgian exteriors. Our house had no Georgian front but had been left untouched at the end of the churchyard, under the shadow of St. Mary's church, three slumped storeys of fourteenth-century lath, plaster, and beam, with a crazily gabled porch.

There were cellars under the house and three blanked-off wells. The cellars have walls of dripping flint, ancient disused fireplaces, and cupboards. Though I have seen them recently and marvelled to find them small I cannot tell how old they are. Once there was a south window in the cellars but now only the rotting sill is left, a beam crushed in the wall. My father amiably rigged me a swing in one dark corner for use on rainy days but I never used it unless he was there — never dared to stay alone with the gloom and the crushed wood underground, where a footfall overhead seemed to come down out of another world. So old were the cellars that they must have been dug before the graveyard a few feet away; must pre-date the graves. In those days I hoped they pre-dated the graveyard but could not be sure. In daylight the chances were even or perhaps more favourable than that.

We had a garden at the back of the house, not large, but with lawn, flowers, and a few trees. In daylight the trees leaned out over the churchyard or over the path through it and the stones were nothing but stones. But as the sun went down behind the church tower, the stones became stiller than stone — as if they were waiting. When the sun had gone down I did not look at the churchyard at all. I knew how the stones were lengthening, lifting and peering blankly, inscrutably, over the wall. As I went indoors, if I dared a backward glance, or climbed towards the little shot window, I saw how they did indeed peer; but up, always over my shoulder or my head, crowded, still, other. Then I would go quickly to my father or my mother or my brother for human company by the fire.

One afternoon I was sitting on the wall that divided our garden from the churchyard. Eight, was I, perhaps, or nine? Or older even? There is nothing by which I can tell. I contemplated the stones a few feet away and saw suddenly that several of them were flat up against our wall. I remember knowing then that I had seen and thought enough. My nights were miserable as it was, with every sort of apprehension given a label, and these even so only outliers of a central, not-comprehended dark. But the sun shone on the wall and I watched the inside of my head go on and take step after logical step. At which end of a grave does a stone stand? I remembered the sexton, Mr. Baker, calling them headstones and I made the final deduction that the dead lay, their heads under our wall, the rest of them projecting from their own place into our garden, their feet, their knees even, tucked under our lawn.

Logic is insistent. I recall an awareness at that moment that I was being foolish; that the demonstration of this proposition would do no one any good and me a great deal of harm. The lawn, almost the only uncontaminated place in that ancient neighbourhood, had been sunny and innocent until my deliberate exercise of logic had invited the enemy in.

What was that enemy? I cannot tell. He came with darkness and he reduced me to a shuddering terror that was incurable because it was indescribable. In daylight I thought of the Roman remains that had been dug up under the church as the oldest things near, sane things from sane people like myself. But at night, the Norman door and pillar, even the flint wall of our cellar, were older, far older, were rooted in the darkness under the earth.

I guess now at causes for all these terrors. Had my mother perhaps feared this shadowy house and its graveyard neighbour when she went there, with me as a baby? She was Cornish and the Cornish do not live next to a graveyard from choice. But we had very little choice. My father was a master at the local grammar school so that we were all the poorer for our respectability.

In the dreadful English scheme of things at that time, a scheme which so accepted social snobbery as to elevate it to an instinct, we had our subtle place. Those unbelievable gradations ensured that though my parents could not afford to send my brother and me to a public school, we should nevertheless go to a grammar school. Moreover we must not go first to an elementary school but to a dame school where the children were nicer though the education was not so good. In fact, like everybody except the very high and the very low in those days, we walked a social tightrope, could not mix with the riotous children who made such a noise and played such wonderful games on the Green. I did not question these contradictions.

But at eight or nine the standard of education did not matter. My father could see to that. He was incarnate omniscience. I have never met anybody who could do so much, was interested in so much, and who knew so much. He could carve a mantelpiece or a jewel box, explain the calculus and the ablative absolute. He wrote a textbook of geography, of physics, of chemistry, of botany and zoology, devised a course in astronavigation, played the violin, the 'cello, viola, piano, flute. He painted expertly, knew so much about flowers he denied me the simple pleasure of looking anything up for myself. He produced a cosmology which I should dearly love to pass off as all my own work because he never told anyone but me about it. He fell hideously and passionately in love with wireless in the very earliest days and erected an aerial like the one on a battleship, and had some unused qualifications as an architect. He hated nothing in the whole world unless it were a tory, and then only as a matter of principle and on academic lines. He stumped the country for the Labour Party, telling the farm labourers that the Labour Party did not want to exploit the workers the way the tories did; it simply wanted to do away with them. He stood proudly and indignantly with my mother on the town hall steps under the suffragette banner, and welcomed the over-ripe tomatoes. He inhabited a world of sanity and logic and fascination. He found life so busy and interesting that he had no time for a career at all. But that was all right. His children would have the career in his place and restore the balance of nature. He and my mother brought us up with a serious care which he gave to nothing else but wireless and politics.

Sitting on the garden wall, then, it was a voice from this world that shouted to me as I pondered on the trap of darkness that was closing. The interruption was too late, for my logical process was complete. So I let myself down, and ran indoors as my brother began to shout as well. They were in the hall, grouped round the tangle of wire and tin and glass bulbs that was now my father's obsession. My mother stood with earphones on and she was looking inside her head. 'Listen!' said my brother, 'let him listen!'

My mother looked out, lifted off one earphone so that I could listen too. I put my ear to the damp vulcanite, pressed my ear in against the soft iron diaphragm. My father and brother gazed at me and held their breath. Yes. No illusion, this. Sure enough, there were sounds in the earphone. There had been sounds before on some occasions — a frying noise usually, and once a chirping which drove my father into mad excitement because he said it was morse from a ship. But now, in the deep fat, covered over, browned, there was a tiny structure of noise which tickled my ear without particularly interesting it. I listened and waited for something to happen.

My father whispered impatiently against my disengaged ear. 'It's a violin!'

Astonished, I saw that my father was different. His usually pink and white face was now white all over. He was sweating, large drops were trickling down the enormous dome of his head. He was shaking with a depth of emotion that I myself only experienced round about midnight. He bent down and whispered to me out of his world, out of sanity and order, out of boundless hope; out of a torn-up sense of the miracle: 'You may never hear a violinist as good as that again!'

My mother lifted her aquiline, capable face away from the headphones. She looked at my father a shade severely, as though the miracle, once performed, had no business not to continue. 'What are you doing, Alec? It's fading away!'

My father leapt to the hall table where our machinery was. He lifted a row of electrodes out of their solution and held them so, waiting for the battery to recover. We stood, dedicated. He lowered them again. My brother shook his head: 'It's gone.'

And so it was. Weeks of gloom were to pass before the wireless brought us another off-hand miracle — years before my distraught father won through to serenity and had the machinery tamed, the house wired, and music falling from the air. On that first day, I left him wrestling and muttering over the mess and returned to the contaminated garden.

How could I talk to them about darkness and the irrational? They knew so much, had such certainties, were backing all the obvious winners. I floated in their world, holding on to a casual hand, sometimes sinking again in the dark. Then I found Edgar Allan Poe's *Tales of Mystery and Imagination*. I read them with a sort of shackled fascination and recognized their quality, knew they were reports, knew that he and I had been in the same place.

There was of course an escape. From such an impasse, we escape or die or go mad. I had respite from my obsessions. I climbed away from them. Coming along the churchyard from St. Mary's beneath the avenue of pollarded limes, you find the wall on the left heightens suddenly. That was the wall of our garden and we had a chestnut tree which stood in that corner. I cut it down a few years ago with strangely little regret. Now that the lawn was distasteful I learned to climb that tree with a kind of absent-minded dexterity. There is something about a tree which appeals not to a vestigial instinct but to the most human, if you like the highest, in a child. The tree to be preferred is rooted in a garden or among houses. In a forest a tree is no wilder than the ground; is nothing but a single hair on the world's head. Just as a boat attracts in the contrary way by being a house in the savagery of water, so a tree is a bit of the Congo or Antarctica set down next to the paving stones or main drain. Everything else has been shaped, touched, used and understood, plumbed, by powerful adults. But a tree lifts its fork above them, ramifies in secret. There is in a tree only a yard or two over your head, that which is most precious to a small boy; an unvisited place, never seen before, never touched by the hand of man.

This chestnut tree was my escape. Here, neither the darkness of the churchyard nor this vast pattern of work and career and importance could get at me. The texture of bark, the heraldic shapes of stick buds, these were private, were an innocent reality, were in fact nothing but themselves. Here, stirring the leaves aside, I could look down at the strangers in that world from which we were cut off and reflect on their nature. Safe from skeletons, from Latin and the proper requirements of growing up, I could ponder over or snigger at the snatches of conversation from passers-by underneath. There were two little girls who came along, patter, patter, through a deserted churchyard and a bright afternoon. One was thin and dark and awe-stricken and excited. The other was fair, a little bigger, giggling and self-appalled. She was leaning down sideways, explaining. As she passed, her voice came into tune.

'They gets you down and pulls off your clothes.'

Giggle away under the trees. Gone. What a fierce and dramatic life these girls must lead in their own place, I thought! How cruelly inhuman their treatment of each other! Then the old bookie passed. He was short, grey, and square as a sarsen stone. He came from the pubs at three o'clock in the afternoon. He inched along the path, with shuffling steps each no more than a span, or less. He inched along, swearing to himself, inscrutably angry, muttering. He would stop, strike at the stone walls with his stick and inch on. There was that other pair too, a man and a woman. They stopped below me one evening when the late light of summer and a full moon had encouraged me to brave the shadows and stay in my tree until night. Even the moonlight was hot, molten moonlight, a great dollop of white moon stirred by the twigs and leaves into a shower of moving drops. These two, the man and woman, stood by the wall under me, she against it, he pressing her hard, and they wrestled and murmured gently. She would take her mouth away from his face and say 'no, no, no', and put it back again. His moony hand was in her neck. Then he began to undo something near her neck and she said 'no, no, no', more earnestly and laughed and giggled. But his hand went into her chest and she gave a gasp of pain like being pricked with a pin or having something raw touched, and the branch I was holding aside flicked back with a swish. They started apart and stood looking up at me, or at the covering leaves only a yard away. She said: 'What was that?' He said: 'It was a bird' — and his voice had a lot of heart-beat and phlegm in it. But there were footsteps coming past St. Mary's now. The man and woman hurried away.

But these encounters, real and innocent as the chestnut tree, lives devoid of darkness or career, were still beside the point. I enjoyed their quality but had no theories about them. They were pictures, put away by me then, to be taken out and evaluated later. The tree also let me read what I liked, avidly and uncritically. Crouched in the branches, lifted above fear, I had no doubt that if one frowned long enough at the page it would brighten and come alive. Indeed, it did. The words and paper vanished. The picture emerged. Details were there to be heard, seen, touched. Percival's sister let down her long hair from the abbey gate and it swayed gently like virginia creeper because there was a slight breeze. Pius Aeneas had a stiff neck for three days after he carried old Anchises from burning Troy. He carried him, of course, with one leg over each shoulder, as my father had carried me. I know something about Odysseus that is not in the text, since I have seen and touched him. When he was washed up in Phaeacia his hands were white and corrugated and his nails bled — not because of the rocks but because he bit them. I saw him, crouched naked beneath the stunted olive, shuddering in the wind, salt drying on his skin, lugging with white teeth at the nail of his third right finger while he peered at the dark, phantom dangers and wondered fearfully what to do. The wily, the great-hearted, the traveller, the nail-biter.

These moving pictures in Technicolor lit the underside of the leaves. This place was where I lived. Among our few acquaintances I became a sight. People were led to the garden and I was pointed out to them, like a rare bird. My father, kind as ever, even made me a short ladder which would enable me, and anyone else who was so inclined, to climb the tree easily. That ladder was difficult to break but the effort was well repaid. The tree, hardly to be distinguished in my mind from the moving pictures, remained inviolate.

But down in the house rooted in the graveyard, things were moving forward. The time had now come when the first steps towards a career must be taken. Yet it was observed I resisted school or, rather, let it flow over me. There was Latin, for example. You could not go to Oxford unless you learnt Latin. On the other hand Latin was useless except to scholars. But my career was to be a scientific one. Science was busy clearing up the universe. There was no place in this exquisitely logical universe for the terrors of darkness. There was darkness, of course, but it was just darkness, the absence of light; had none of the looming terror which I knew night-long in my very bones. God might have been a help but we had thrown Him out, along with Imperialism, Toryism, the Exploitation of Women, War and the Church of England. I nodded agreement, was precocious with the catch-phrases of progress; but even in daylight now, the dead under the wall drew up the green coverlet of our grass and lay back with a heart-squeezing grin. Though cosmology was driving away the shadows of our ignorance, though bones were exhibited under glass, though the march of science was irresistible, its path did not lie through my particular darkness. One day I should be part of that organization marching irresistibly to a place which I was assured was worth finding. The way to it lay through a net of Latin's golden, bumbling words. But Latin marched away from me. I had a divinatory skill in translation but the grammar seemed related to nothing in any universe and I left it alone.

My father was appalled and, I think, frightened. 'You've got brains — I know you've got brains!' But not for Latin grammar.

'It doesn't need intelligence, you know — just sticking at it! And you can stick at things — look at the books you read! You can stick at it!' Not Latin grammar.

'But you've got brains!' No.

'Now look. I'll explain it again!' No use. No go.

I knew I could not learn Latin grammar for a perfectly clear reason, a logical reason. The logic of childhood is just as good as adult logic — better sometimes, because unconditioned. Logic is only a few different shaped bricks, after all, out of which we build skyscrapers. But in childhood the axioms are different. I had an adventure book and the word 'Latin' occurred on page 67. At some time a blot of ink had fallen on that page and blotted out the word 'Latin!'. I knew that in my universe, though not in my father's, this was enough. I should never be able to learn Latin.

'Haven't you got any brains, then?' No use. Not for Latin grammar. No go.

He never knew. No one else knew.

There came a time when I got no marks at all in a Latin test and minus one for bad writing. Then we had a show down.

Let me make one point perfectly clear. My father was generous, loving, saintly in his attitude to his family. He would give up anything for us gladly. He was understanding, too. His human stature grows, the more I think of him. If we could not meet at this point it was no failing of his. It seems more like a defect in the nature of human communication.

What I remember most of that terrible evening is the reasonableness of my father's arguments. If I really did not want to go to Oxford, that was all right. If I would prefer to go into the Merchant Navy, that was all right. If I wanted to leave school at fourteen, that was all right too. Now please don't cry, I don't like it when you cry! It you want to forget the whole thing, that's all right. Everything was all right, in fact. Then why do I remember such anguish, such tears, such sobs racking up from the soles of my feet, mouth agape, sweat, streaming nose, mouth, and eyes, misery, hopeless misery? When I could cry no more, I lay, my face a few inches from the white skirting of the hall, and jerked and sniffed and shuddered. I was, I saw, in a place. Just as I had recognized that Poe and I knew a place which we shared, so now I knew this place, this atmosphere. It was real, grey, had the quality of promising a dreary familiarity. It was the first step on the road. I saw that I should really do this thing, really learn Latin and grow up.

I moved, sniffing, to the dining-room and sat down with Richie's *First Steps in Latin*, and Richie's *Second Steps*. I needed to begin at the beginning. My father and mother sat on either side of the fire and hardly breathed. I thumbed the books through. Rules, declensions, paradigms and vocabularies stretched before me. They were like a ladder which I knew now I should climb, rung after factual rung, and Sir James Jeans and Professor Einstein were waiting at the top to sign me on. I was glad about science in a remote sort of way. If you were going to be anything, then a scientist was what you ought to be. But the ladder was so long. In this dreary mood of personal knowledge and prophecy I knew that I should climb it; knew too that the darkness was all around, inexplicable, unexorcized, haunted, a gulf across which the ladder lay without reaching to the light.

My parents must have been emotionally exhausted. They stayed quiet and I worked for two and a half hours. I found, as in the last hour or two I had expected, that I could learn the stuff and that it was ridiculously easy. I moved on, surely and quietly, from rung to rung over the dark. My mother came at last and stood by my side and put her arm round me. 'It's not so bad when you get started, is it?' No. Not so bad.

All at once, the air became light and jolly. We cracked jokes. We laughed. *Amemus*. My father put away his book on Vertebrate Zoology. 'Go on like this', he cried delightedly, 'and we shall find we have to stop you doing too much Latin!'

'The next thing', said my mother, 'and he'll be taking his Latin up the tree!'